Immortal Wine:
The First Born

Immortal Wine: The First Born

A novel by
Andy Elliott

Strategic Book Publishing and Rights Co.

Copyright © 2016 Andy Elliott. All rights reserved.

No part of this book may be reproduced or transmitted in any form or by any means, graphic, electronic, or mechanical, including photocopying, recording, taping, or by any information storage retrieval system, without the permission, in writing, of the publisher. For more information, send an email to support@sbpra.net, Attention Subsidiary Rights Department.

Strategic Book Publishing & Rights Co., LLC
USA | Singapore
www.sbpra.com

For information about special discounts for bulk purchases please contact Strategic Book Publishing and Rights Co. Special Sales at bookorder@sbpra.net.

ISBN: 978-1-68181-606-7

ALSO BY ANDY ELLIOTT

NONFICTION

A Practical Guide for Personal Support Workers from a P.S.W. Volume 1

ISBIN: 978-1-62212-356-8

Dedication

I am dedicating this book to all the people who enjoy a quality horror/suspense story. There are some great ones out there. May this also become one of them! This book is also dedicated to my loyal readers. Even though I've changed the subject matter, it's nice to keep your support. Also as always to my loving wife Wanda, and my four beautiful daughters; Harley, Mackayla, Katherine, and Nikita... May all your dreams come true, and for me to remain the scariest thing in your rooms.

Enjoy!

Acknowledgments

I would like to take this opportunity to thank the awesome people who helped me make this work of fiction into the book it is today. Without the feedback, advice, and encouragement from my Purple Party sisters; the chosen few who proof read my manuscript prior to it becoming this book, and the support from my wife and children this book would still be sitting in manuscript form hidden in a computer file on my laptop.

I also have to thank my publisher for having enough confidence in my manuscript to believe that it was good enough for Strategic Publishing to make it into book form, as well as providing the guidance and feedback that I, as a new novelist, needed to produce a well-polished finished product—and for pointing out the added value of consulting with one of their editors to turn this once roughly formed gem into the diamond it now is.

Last but not least I have also need to thank my "Ink Master", Joe "Brigadeir" Martin. Your wicked illustrations help turn these pages into a true work of art. You are a god amongst men.

Table of Contents

Storeroom	1
Chase	11
Home Coming	19
Gail	27
Home	34
Immortal Wine	47
Awakening	56
Origins	78
Destiny	99
Vladimir	112
Enlightenment	125
Something In Blue	138
Bitter Truths	148

Introduction

Life changed for Chase twenty-five years ago, following a senseless accident. That resulted in the death of his mother.

Chase left his family home shortly following his mothers' funeral, and hadn't returned since.

After a ten hour shift at the mill, where he worked six days a week. Chase returned to the single room he lived in, at a run-down boarding house three blocks away from the mill. Entering the room he found an envelope lying on the floor, inside his room. He picked it up in the dark and walked across the room to sit on the single bed. As tired as he was from the long day at work, he was compelled to open the letter to find out who it was from.

With a dread filled heart he tore the envelope open and read the letter inside. The letter was from his father. A man he had not seen nor spoke to in twenty-five years.

Chase had to read the letter three times before the words within it sunk in. His dread filled heart turned to ice. He had to return home!

In the process of trying to decide what to do, now that his life had once more been turned upside down, Chase ran into an old flame. Causing him even more confusion; and heartache with the return of his childhood love.

Chase made a startling discovery that forever changed his life. That all began by stumbling across an ancient chest, covered with countless years for dirt, and grim.

Prescript

I entered into this piece of work because I like you, enjoy a good story. Whereas I've read a large number of author's works. Stephen King has always been and will always be my all-time favorite. You might see some of my affection for his works in my writing style herein. However I strive to have a flavor all to myself.

This being my first work of fiction might come as a shock to those of you who have read my other book in the past. But suck it up people. I have never claimed to be one sided, nor would I want to be that boring. Face it I've been accused of having a warped mind. Within these pages you'll find a little bit that has seeped out.

I promise to try not to bore you with this story. I'll strive to keep it action packed and compelling enough to keep you wanting more. After all the things that go bump in the night should keep you awake, not put you to sleep. So sit back, get comfy. Enjoy your time within the folds of my over burdened mind.

Oh, and never mind that little noise you just heard outside your window, it's only Chase wanting to come inside.

Disclaimer

This book is a work of fiction. Names, characters, places, and incidents either are products of the author's imagination or are used fictionally. Any resemblance to actual events or locales or persons, living, dead or un-dead, is entirely coincidental.

Storeroom

As the sun was setting on another smoking hot July day, a stiff breeze blew from the East. Sending yet another; blinding curtain of gritty sand along the hard packed, rutted dirt roads of Snarleyville, Ontario.

Although it was only running into dark, the street was almost empty. The few people out and about, were heading to their destination quickly with their heads down and their scarves drawn tight over their nose and mouths. In order to keep out the majority of the dry grit, all the storefronts were boarded up tight for the night. With the exception of the carriage house, the bunk house, a couple of hotel's, the inn, and a few scattered bars.

Lone Moon Coach House was in full swing. Proving to be, the single most popular watering hole in town; once again. With the temperatures heading into the low hundred's as the day marched along, there was hardly an empty seat in the bar. Norman the owner/barkeep was manning his post behind the bar as usual. His wife Wilma was running drinks to the out laying tables.

Norman was shrewd and watchful of his customers. Standing at five foot nine inches tall, weighing one hundred ninety-five pounds. Most people looked at him and didn't want to upset him. Although Norman was pushing sixty, he was still well built for his age. His reputation for busting heads for the slightest commotion helped keep his patrons in line.

Wilma on the other hand had a reputation of being a little loose of morals, though not many people were brave enough to let Norman hear this from them. Wilma was eighteen years younger than Norman. As of yesterday July 13, 1852 they had been married for ten years. Wilma still retained some of her younger slender figure. She was five foot three inches tall and only weighed in at one hundred and twenty pounds. Although she had to admit she was getting a little thicker about the middle. She still turned heads as she moved around the room. As she shifted through the room swishing her long skirts, she took special care to ensure she rubbed up against the "big tippers".

Little did Norman know but Wilma made majority of her hefty tips by taking select customers back into the storage room with her. As she looked around the room she noted a good number of her "regulars", and figured she'd be making an extra fifty dollars in "tips" tonight. Of course Norman knew nothing of her "tips"; she had a special little hiding place for them. Her plan was to one day leave Norman and open a brothel in another town, with more people…and money. Over the past six years she had put away almost ten thousand dollars, all from her loyal customers.

Norman was hammering the spigot into a fresh keg of whiskey when Wilma called to him that she was going to powder her nose.

Norman was too busy tapping the keg to look up and only grunted, "Hurry up about it, we're busier than a fly on a fresh pile of shit tonight".

Had he of looked up he'd have seen Wilma slip into the storeroom with a tall dark haired man wearing a long dusty black range coat.

Wilma turned on the man after swinging the door shut behind them, saying in her regular business voice, "You've got five minutes to spill your seed, then I've got to get back out there before Norman comes looking for me".

Without further ado Wilma turned away from the man, leaned over a case of sarsaparilla, and hiked her skirts up over her hips. Wilma never was one for wearing bloomers, so once her full length skirts were above her hips. Her entire lower end was bare and fully exposed to her gentleman's hungry eyes. Not wanting to waste any time Wilma urged him to get on with it, from her roost. Breaking free of the trance Wilma's bare bottom had cast him into. The man quickly freed his stiffening manhood from his trousers as he watched her wiggle her hips suggestively at him. Within seconds the man was pounding into her fast, deep and hard. As this wasn't a new arrangement between them the man already knew the rules. He could spill his seed but not inside her, because if she got pregnant she'd be dead. Norman was unable to sire children after a riding accident that nearly claimed his life when he was thirty. He felt himself nearing the point of finally spilling his seed. He told her he was almost finished. Wilma quickly slid free from him and closed her hand over his manhood. She dropped to her knees and took him in her mouth, just as he let loose and flooded her hungry mouth.

Afterwards while fixing their cloths back into place Wilma collected her usual two dollars before exiting the storeroom. Sure it was a hefty sum of money, but it helped keep an exclusive clientele and she'd proven to be worth every cent of it over the years.

About an hour later Wilma again stated that she "had to powder her nose". This time she slipped into the storeroom with two men, at the same time. Little did she realize that the sarsaparilla had just run out at the bar! Norman held off for as long as he could, then softly cursing Wilma's "weak bladder" under his breath. He went to the storeroom for another case of sarsaparilla.

Norman opened the door, and then stopped mid-step staring in disbelief. Three feet further into the room there was Wilma having sex with two men! Norman briefly witnesses his whore of a wife being pounded back and forth between the two men, and then he only saw red. Without uttering a single word Norman drew his Colt 45 Peacemaker from his hip holster and fired three quick rounds off. The sound within the small room was deafening.

The first shot took Wilma square in the side of her pretty little head. The second shot took the closest man to the door right between the eyes, as he turned towards the source of the deafening noise. He dropped lifeless to the floor. The third and final shot took out the right eye of the man screwing his newly ex-wife from behind. When the third man hit the floor, Norman stepped back and re-closed the door.

Norman returned to the bar without the case of sarsaparilla. Laying his peacemaker on the bar top under the watchful eyes of everyone left breathing in the bar. Norman gently placed a glass beside the gun, and poured a longshot of whiskey. After quickly draining the glass, Norman looked around the bar.

An eternity of tense seconds later Norman blinked his eyes twice and calmly stated, "Jonah, go fetch the sheriff, I just killed three people".

Before Jonah could move Norman said loud enough for everyone in the bar to hear, "Time to go home folks, the bar is closed...likely for good".

After which Jonah quickly left with everyone else. Ten minutes later Jonah returned following the sheriff and five deputies. Wyatt Jameson had only been the sheriff of Snarleyville for two months. He was only a small man, soft spoken and deadly afraid of violence. Though he'd only been the sheriff for two months, Wyatt knew Norman well. They both grew up together, and had even shared a fair number of girls in the process. Wyatt had only took up the sheriff position because it was a quiet town, and it was only suppose to be until the marshal's office could find someone to fill the position. Had he of known two months ago that he would have to arrest one of his oldest friends, he would have refused the position.

Wyatt didn't want to walk over to the bar and arrest Norman, but it was his job and his alone. Wyatt took off his dusty hat, ran a hand through his slippery hair, and slowly walked over to the bar.

Placing his hat on the bar over Norman's peacemaker he said, "Evenin' Norm, I hear you've had a spot of trouble here tonight".

Norman didn't answer other than slowly nodding his head. "Do you wanna talk about it?" asked Wyatt.

Slowly looking up at Wyatt, Norman said, "My whore of a wife was taking two hard stiff ones in the storeroom. I shot the bitch and her two friends too. You might as well set me a date with the long-drop. I did it, I confess".

Wyatt reluctantly walked to the edge of the bar where Norman was standing and said, "Well then you had better turn around, so as I can put these cuffs on you".

Norman slowly turned around and was handcuffed before being lead off to the jail. After securing Norman into a cell Wyatt pulled a bottle of scotch out of the bottom drawer of his desk, along with two glasses. Pouring a long shot into both glasses he returned to the cell and handed one through the bars to Norman.

Looking at the glass in disbelief, Norman accepted it.

Smiling Wyatt said, "It's been one hell of a night, I recon you need this worse than I do, I think".

Norman tipped his head and replied, "Yep, I guess you might be right about that".

Downing the contents of the glasses in quick succession Wyatt said, "You wanna talk about what happened?"

Staring off into the distance Norman said, "I've spent the last fifteen years of my life with her. I never would have guessed she was a whore. But I'm thinking that when I caught her in the act it wasn't her first time at the rodeo. If you can catch meaning of what I'm trying to say to you, and I'm sure you can. Now I'm gonna swing for the bitch, and I guess I'm glad for it. It'll keep me from going insane seeing it all played out again every time I close my eyes".

Wyatt didn't know what to say, so he kept his thoughts to himself. Norman sat quietly for a long time staring at his boots.

Wyatt was just about to stand up when Norman said, "Can I trouble you for something to write with…and on? I'd better set my affairs in order or our good old government is gonna end up with everything I've got".

Wyatt fetched a large chunk of graphite from his desk and a handful of parchment paper.

Handing it over to Norman he stated, "I'll leave the lights on for you. I've gotta give the boys back at the bar, their orders. Then I'm heading home to get some down time. I'll see you in a few hours. Try to get some sleep…once you're done you're… um…writing".

Wyatt left Norman staring off into the unseen distance, and returned to the bar. Wyatt told three of the five deputies to go home for some sleep. He figured the older deputies would be able to handle things on their own. Wyatt told his deputies to wait until the undertaker picked up the bodies. Then lock up the bar and go home for some sleep. Wyatt told his men he was going home for some shut eye, and not to bother him unless it was very, very important. Wyatt left them and slowly headed for home. He couldn't remember ever feeling so drained before in his life.

Walking into his house Wyatt noticed the sky in the distance starting to lighten up in anticipation of the coming morning.

Wyatt wasn't the only one who didn't get much sleep that night. Norman filled five pages of parchment front and back, before folding them in half twice. Taking another piece of parchment he fashioned it into an envelope, before slipping his letter inside it. After a few minutes thought, he slowly printed a name and address onto the front of the envelope.

Setting the graphite and remaining parchment aside, Norman laid the enveloped letter down onto the floor beside the hard stone bed. Laid down and turned towards the cold stone wall. His cell was starting to brighten up as he finally drifted off to sleep.

Norman woke up two hours later when Wyatt returned. Norman asked for some sealing wax to secure the make shift envelope, and was provided with it. The letter was later dropped off at the post office for delivery by Wyatt. Norman was informed later in the evening that he would be hung until dead in three days hence, for the crime of murdering three people in cold blood. Norman was fine with this decision, as he felt he had nothing left to live for. With his whore of a wife now lying dead in a pine box by his own hand; waiting to be planted in the dirt. And his only child, his son; living his own life in some ratty little town hundreds of miles away.

The next day the local undertaker stopped by the jail and measured Norman for his coffin. He was followed shortly after by Burnie the barber, who provided Norman with his final shave and trim.

Laughing Norman said, "I thank you, a man should be looking his best when going to meet his maker".

Burnie wouldn't accept payment from Norman, stating, "I've known you for going on thirty years, I consider you a good friend. As a friend I wanted to do this for you. It's a shame what's going to happen, but I understand why you did what you did."

Michael stopped by the jail on the second day, to measure Norman for his last suit.

As he was walking back out the door he said over his shoulder, "I hope she is in hell, and is happy there. You're a good man and deserve better than what she's cost ya. I'll see you tomorrow with your suit. And don't even bother insulting me then or now trying to pay me for it, I'll have none of it".

On the day of the drop Michael returned good to his word shortly after ten a.m. with Normans' suit.

Staying long enough to ensure it fit properly, Michael said, "If I'd had of know what she was up to I'd have done the deed for you, you're a good man. Me not so much, it doesn't seem right for you to take the drop when I'm staying above ground".

With his eye's misting over Michael left the jail, never to return.

The gallows were finished being built shortly after two p.m. Norman was scheduled to take the plunge at five p.m. He was led out of the jail at exactly ten to five. Wyatt asked him if he had anything he wanted to say before time ran out.

Smiling Norman said, "I've said all the words I needed to say; now I'm ready for the endless sleep. Let's get this deed done so people can move on".

The hangman lowered the hood into place over Normans' head. Placed the rope around Normans' neck, and then tightened it up. When the town clock began to chime five p.m. the hangman pulled the lever he was standing next to. Before the clock stopped ringing Norman was gone from the world, leaving only his cooling body to be tended to.

The rope was cut loose after Jason the millers son had grabbed ahold of Normans' legs to stop him from slamming into the ground when cut loose. Norman had he been willing to look, might have been surprised to see the attendance of his short hanging. Present were only Wyatt the sheriff, the hangman, the undertaker, and Jason. No one wanted to watch their friend hang. Not even the ones who had been screwing his wife in the storeroom for the past six years. Or anywhere else they met up to screw.

Norman was buried in the cemetery on the outside of town. Unfortunately as he'd killed three people he was banned from the Catholic cemetery. However his friends buried him as close to it as they could. As the sun went down on that fateful third day, the last shovel full of dirt was slowly dumped into place on Norman's grave.

As the last shovel was tossed into the back of the undertaker's wagon, Wyatt pulled a small flask of whisky from his pocket and said, "One last drink with you, old friend".

As he opened the flask took a long haul then up ended it over the fresh grave, pouring the remaining liquor onto the fresh dirt.

The next morning Norman's final letter arrived at its intended address. The recipient his only son from a previous marriage would get it eight hours later, when he returned home from working at the mill.

Andy Elliott

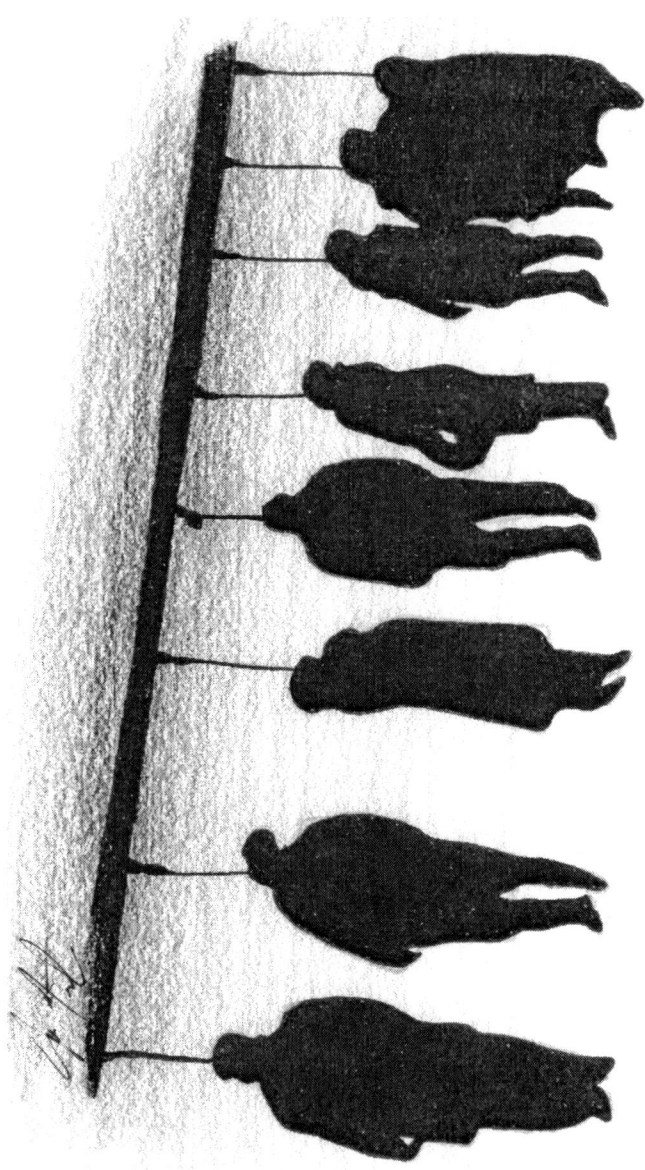

Chase

The harsh shrill whistle sounded throughout the mill. Chase turned off the light above his table as the huge grinding wheel next to him, slowly came to a screeching stop.

Straightening his stiff back he shuffled off towards the front of the mill, and the time ledger. Waiting in line for his turn to clock himself out; Chase wondered, not for the first time, if he would be bent over the same old grinding wheel for the rest of his miserable life. Bending over the ledger after looking at the "official time clock", Chase scribbled down the time and his name on the "out" page.

As Chase slowly walked back to his dingy one room hole in the wall, he thought he would go mad if something didn't change soon. If he knew about the letter that was waiting for him he might have had other thoughts. As it were Chase arrived at home ten minutes after leaving the mill.

Chase had left home twenty-five years ago when his mother had been run over in the street by a stampeding wagon. It was a freak accident and couldn't have been avoided. A starving dog had bitten one of the horses on a leg, causing it to bolt, just as his mother was passing in front of it. She never had a chance. As Chase didn't have any interest in working with his father in his bar, he set out to make his own mark on the world. Thinking back he was now old enough to realize that at sixteen years old it was a stupid move.

Two years later he found the job at the mill and the shitty little room to live in. He'd been there ever sense. Thinking back it was nothing like the way he planned his life to be. But as he didn't have any other options, he was content to stick things out for the time being.

Chase stepped into his room and heard the sound of something go skittering across the floor. Looking down he saw the letter. His stomach dropped. He figured it was from his asshole of a landlord demanding he get out, or some other equally messed up crap. Bending down to pick it up, his already over stressed back threatened to give out on him. After retrieving the letter Chase shuffled over to his bed and sat on the edge of it. Rubbing a kink out of his lower back Chase thought, not for the first time about finding a better job. Being only forty-one years old, he was too young to be hobbling around like an old man.

The envelope had no return address on it. The only markings on it were his name and address, and the cancellation mark over the stamp. Turning the envelope over he seen a large drop of crimson red wax sealing the envelope closed. There was no signet marking the wax to offer any insight into the identity of the sender. Breaking the seal Chase drew out the folded pages and opened them up.

Chase immediately recognized the hand writing as his father's. His heart thudded loudly in his chest and his stomach clenched. He hadn't heard from his father since he moved out. This was a bad omen. In the dim light of his room Chase turned on the light beside his bed, not that it brightened things up much. Leaning back against the wall Chase read his father's letter.

Chase

I know we haven't talked nor seen each other for many years. Though I owe you the truth, and I wanted you to hear this from me. By the time you receive this letter I will once again be with your mother. As I've no idea if this will be good or bad news for you, I thought I should be the one to tell you.

I know you've had a hard time of things since your mother was killed all those years ago. Even though we haven't talked I have kept an eye on you. I know you're working in that shitty little mill. I know your living in that little one room, at Tomas Green's rooming house. I wish I could have been able to of kept you here with me. Though I understand why you felt you needed to move away from here.

Little comfort to you but your mother truly would have been very proud of you for being the man you have grown into. And also for being a strong enough man to move on with your life after her death. I only wish I had your strength. I mopped around for ten years. I drank myself into a hole and back out of it again, far too many times to count. I almost lost the bar and the house with my selfish self pity and grief. I lost touch with everything for a while, even you.

Then I met Wilma and fell in love with her, and finally married her five years later. Things were going good with us. The bar was back in the black, and I was making good money running it again. Wilma made me happy, and I thought I was making her happy. Though she was not your mother, she almost made me feel as good as she had. Even though she was eighteen years younger than me, as I later found out.

Well earlier today I walked into the storeroom to fetch a case of sarsaparilla. That was when I found her with two guys pumping her back and forth between them. Like a saw working to cut down a thick oak tree. I saw red and shot all three of them then and there, before they could even separate themselves from each other. Hell I doubt they even knew I found them until I shot them. Then I turned myself into the sheriff. I will be hung 'til I'm dead in three days' time.

I don't know if you would have come to watch if you knew in time or not. But as I do love you, I wanted to spare you from having to see it. I likely could have talked the sheriff into postponing until you could be here. But like I said, I love you too much to let you see me swinging from the end of a rope.

That being said I leave the bar and house to you. You can do with them as you wish. I know you didn't want anything to do with the bar and likely still don't. You should be able to fetch a good price for it, if you decide to sell it. It is fully stocked right now as I just had a liquor delivery yesterday, and only sold around three hundred dollars worth of booze. So long as you decide to come home to it you can keep it and get drunk, sell it, or do with it as you wish. That leaves the house. Everything inside it is yours as well. So you know there are some very valuable items inside it. You will find a small steel chest inside my bedroom closet with a list and value of those items. There are also a number of deeds in it that I have collected over the years, by one way or another. They are yours now too. I have no idea if any of them are worth much. Hell to be honest I never really had any interest in them, nor do I even remember how many are there. However they are deeds to various properties. So if nothing else, they could always be sold off if you don't want them either.

There is also a safe in the den (your old bedroom) with some gold, cash, and diamonds in it. The combination of the safe will be easy for you to remember, as it is your birthday. There is also a large and valuable wine collection in the cellar. The last time I remember taking stock; there were three thousand bottles down there. However there may be considerably more than that down there now. I haven't really been doing much with it in the past number of years since you left home other than adding bottles as they come to me. On the work table in the same room you will see a black ledger book. This contains the name, year, and value of every bottle in the collection (at least at the time I logged them into the book), as I added them to my collection. I have not made an entry in it for the twenty-five years; since you left home. So it is only a partial list at best.

This will aid you if you decide to sell them, as I know you likely have no idea what they are worth, nor should that be a reason for you to get ripped off if you do decide to sell them. Oh, I just remembered there is also a metal chest (at least I think it is metal, it has been a number of years since I last looked at it) in the cellar. It is locked with an old dirty lock. I never had the key for it, so far as I know and never got around to getting it opened. I have no idea what is in it, as it was already there when I bought the house. Only god knows how old it is, or for that matter who left it there. Hell I never even moved it from where it was left. So it may be full to bursting or only contain stale air. I hope you can find it in your heart to forgive me for not being the father you deserved to have.

I hope you can find some enjoyment, or use in the things I've left you. If nothing else, sell it all and you will be set for a very, very long time. I've about run out of time to get this letter finished before the sheriff returns, so I'll end it here.

Just take this letter to Wyatt Jameson, the sheriff here now. It'll be proof enough for him to give you my things he collected from me when he arrested me. The keys for the bar and house are with my things here at the jail. Oh, and you'll get some pocket money too, as I had five hundred dollars on me when I was arrested. I had time to empty the cash box while I was waiting for Wyatt to get to the bar. To arrest me; after sending someone the fetch him, after I kill the three of them. God knows what would have happened to it otherwise, someone might have helped themselves to it.

I wish you well in life, and will continue loving you. I don't know if there is a hereafter or not, but if so I'll wait for you there with your mother.

Take care of yourself, my son...Oh I almost forgot. There are a couple of loose floor boards at the foot of my bed on the far side of the room. I know Wilma has been using it as a hiding spot for her "tips". I don't know if there is anything in it, but you might want to check it out just to be sure. Hell for all I know it could be stuffed to busting with whatever she keeps in there.

With all my heart, and love
Dad

Chase read the entire letter through three times before he could make sense of it. His father and step mother were dead, along with two other men. And his father had killed them all, because he caught her screwing the two men. Remembering his father's quick temper he could see his father shooting them without thinking. It was probably a good thing his father was hung. Else he would have driven himself mad constantly reliving it, as also was his custom.

Though Chase hadn't seen or heard from his father for twenty-five years, it hurt. Chase had loved his father, and had often thought of going back to be with him, or even just to visit him. The only reason he never did was because he didn't want his father to think he was a failure. Now it was too late. He'd never be able to tell his father again that he loved him. The thought of his father confessing he was proud of him hurt more than anything. Knowing even facing death it had cost his father everything to admit it.

In the dim light of that shitty little room Chase cried himself to sleep, thinking of his dead father and returning home one last time. Chase dreamed that he was there when his father walked in on his step-mother and that he watched her die. He could clearly see his father pulling his big gun and shooting them almost as quickly as he opened the door. Chase could even smell the fresh gun powder as clearly as if he were really there. Then his dream jumped forward and he was watching his father swinging from the end of a rope. Chase watched as he twisted from left to right as he slowly swung, from side to side. Chase saw there were only four people there, watching as he was. In his dream state he wished this vision to be true. Somehow this just felt right to Chase, as his father had a lot of friends. As such he knew they wouldn't want to be there to watch him die any more than he would have; had he of known in time to attend.

Jerking awake, Chase opened his eyes on the fading vision of his father being cut down and lowered into a waiting coffin. Chase got off the bed and packed his few possessions. He decided he would let the mill know he was quitting due to his father's death and needing to return home. His boss at the mill said he would deposit his last pay into Chase's bank account, as he did not have enough cash on him to just pay him before he set off for home.

Within an hour Chase was in a coach and heading towards his childhood home, and his uncertain future. He still hadn't decided what he was going to do with the bar and house. Should he keep them or sell them? Oh, what to do.

The trip home would take him eight hours by coach. Knowing there was hard cash waiting for him at the end of the line. Chase spent his last few dollars happily for the coach ride. After all he wanted to get back home as soon as he could. Chase leaned back in his seat and fell into a deep dreamless sleep. The bumping and swaying lulled him nicely. He didn't wake up until the coach stopped in Snarleyville. And the coach driver shook him awake.

Fetching his bag from the back of the coach Chase walked across the road to the sheriff's office, which was attached to the jail. Mounting the steps, he saw an older looking man through the window. Figuring it was the sheriff he walked inside.

Home Coming

The gullwing doors parted and a tall man walked inside. Wyatt was sitting at his desk when the man walked in. Looking up he seen a stranger standing there that looked somewhat familiar. Wyatt took a closer look at the stranger to see if he could figure out who he was. Something was nagging the back of his mind, but it refused to form itself into a conscious idea. Though Wyatt knew he should know who this stranger was…was he even a stranger, or did he know him from the past?

The stranger looked to be around six feet four inches tall, slender in build, with long dirty blond hair. He was dressed in faded black jeans, a button up black western style shirt, black cowboy boots, a black cowboy hat that suited him well, and an ankle length black leather trail coat.

Smiling, Wyatt said, "Can I help you stranger?"

Chase walked over to the desk and said, "I'm looking for the sheriff, um, Wyatt Jameson, I believe his name is!"

Leaning back in his chair smiling, Wyatt said, "Well you've come to the right place, I'm Wyatt. What can I do for you?"

Chase told Wyatt who he was and showed him the envelope containing his father's letter, to prove his claim. Wyatt felt like a switch slammed home within his head. Of course he knew this man. Although it had been twenty-five years since Wyatt had last laid eyes upon him. He was definitely a younger version of Norman.

Watching Chase replace the letter in a pocket inside his dusty coat, Wyatt's smile melted from his face. Shaking his head, Wyatt told Chase he was sorry he had to hang his father, but the law was the law and he had no choice. Chase assured the sheriff that both he and his father had always believed in the law. And that they wouldn't have expected the sheriff to have done anything different given the facts of the matter.

Getting up from his desk and crossing the room to a closed door Wyatt said over his shoulder, "Then I guess these things are yours".

Opening the door Wyatt reviled a large safe. With his back to Chase, Wyatt quickly spun the dial left and right entering the combination, and unlocking the large heavy door. Opening the door Wyatt pulled out a small box and handed it to Chase.

Stating, "These are the things your father had on him when I picked him up".

Chase accepted the box and turned to leave.

Before he got more than a step towards the door, Wyatt said, "Just a minute son. This box belongs to you as well. These are the things Wilma had on her, when…ah, well…when she died".

Chase reluctantly accepted the second box. Then turned and headed for the door, and outside. Half way to the door he stopped and turned around.

Smiling he said, "You know it's nice to know you thought of the old man as a friend".

Before turning back to the door and quickly leaving.

Chase sat in the chair outside the sheriff's office with the boxes in his lap. People passed by on the busy street going both ways without paying Chase any attention. After watching them come and go for almost an hour Chase opened the first small box, and looked inside. Other than a bundle of cash held together by a gold money clip, a set of keys, and an ancient looking flip top lighter the box was empty. Chase transferred these items to his pockets.

Seconds later Chase had also emptied the second box into his pockets. It had only contained a couple handfuls of coins, what had been his mother's wedding ring, a pair of small earrings, and a gold necklace. The necklace held a fair sized cross pendant. Obviously the contents of the second box were the remains from his father's dead second wife. Setting the empty boxes on the chair, Chase then wandered off towards what was now his bar.

The walk was a short one as the bar was virtually across the street from the jail. Using one of the keys from the key ring that was in the box, Chase unlocked the door and slipped inside. It wasn't hard to tell that the bar had been closed up and secured quickly the last time it was open. As there were still partially empty glasses and beer bottles littering the table tops and the bar top. After turning on some lights Chase was able to see the storeroom across the floor. The door was still open and there was a large area of the floor covered with congealed blood.

Not wanting to deal with that yet, Chase wandered over to the bar and slipped behind it. He took a beer from the fridge, opened it and took a long drink from the bottle. After setting the bottle on the bar top he opened the cashbox to see what was inside. Expecting to find it empty, as his father had told him had has emptied it in his letter. A quick count of the contents disclosed eight hundred and fifty three dollars and seventy-five cents. Pocketing the money Chase looked around the bar and seriously thought about what he was going to do with the place for the first time since he came into ownership of it. Something didn't make sense to Chase. He could have sworn his father said in his letter that he had emptied the cash box. Pulling the letter from his pocket he quickly skimmed through it until he found the part about the cash box. His father HAD said he emptied it.

So where did this cash come from? Chase made a mental note to ask the sheriff if he knew where it came from.

As he was looking around he came across a ledger on a shelf under the bar. Opening it up and reading through it disclosed that there were some rather valuable bottles of wine, and whiskey being stored inside the bar. Approximately three thousand dollars worth alone just in six single bottles of whiskey, who would have guessed whiskey, could be so valuable? After a rough calculation of how heavy the six bottles would be and the distance from the bar to what used to be his father's house. Chase decided to load the bottles into a crate and take them with him. He would have to make a few additional trips just to get the other valuable bottles listed in the journal, and take them to the house for safer storage of them.

After locating and crating up the bottles Chase left them on the floor inside the door, and exited the bar. Locking the door, he returned to the sheriff's office. Chase informed the sheriff that he would likely be selling the bar as he had no desires to run the place. Also that he would likely be selling the house too once he had a chance to go through them and decide if there was anything he wanted to keep out of them.

The sheriff told Chase where he could go to find someone to sell the bar for him, and the house if and when he was ready to sell them. Chase asked the sheriff if he knew where the money in the cash box had come from.

Wyatt said with a sheepish smile, "A number of people in town had a credit with your dad. They didn't feel right about not settling their accounts. They gave me the money they owed him. As I'd already made an official report of what he had on him when he was arrested. I couldn't add it to it. I figured the only thing I could do with it was put it in the cash box at the bar".

Chase thanked the sheriff and went to the realtor's office. As it was getting to be late in the day the only person in the realtors office was a young lady, named Anna Herth.

Anna told Chase that it was Thomas Dogan's office. And that he was gone for the week on vacation. Chase informed her that he had just come into possession of the bar and a house. He further told her that he would likely want to sell them both in the next little while. He asked her if she could set up an appointment with Thomas to discuss the matter.

Anna further told Chase that if he wanted she could appraise the properties for him if he wished her to. Chase told her he was just heading back to the bar and then off to the house. He told her that he could meet her later in the week, and go over the properties with her. She agreed to meet him at the bar in two days time at nine a.m. Anna told Chase she would wait there for him until ten a.m. if he was not there by then, she'd know he had decided not to sell the properties. Chase thought this was a fine idea as he was still unsure if he was even going to sell them. After the meeting was set up Chase returned to the bar long enough to collect his crate before heading for his old house. Drawing nearer Chase has a strong sense of nostalgia. The house looked the same as the last time he'd seen it, other than a resent coat of paint. And the little tree in the front yard wasn't quite so little any more.

Chase walked up onto the porch and set the crate down.

As he was fishing the key ring from his pocket he heard a soft female voice behind him say, "Chase…Chase is that really you?"

Turning around he saw a pretty strawberry blonde lady standing there. Trying to put a name to her face as he took in her features, Chase was at a loss. He couldn't think of whom this five foot five inch, small boned, sexy looking lady could be.

His confusion must have been apparent on his face because she said, "You don't remember me do you Chase? I'm Gail…do you remember me now?"

Just like a round clicking into place in his old revolver, a flood of memories and emotions crashed down over him. Of course he remembered her. Hell she was his first and last girlfriend in this shitty little town before he moved away. The last time he'd seen her was all those years ago when they were both little more than kids standing on her front porch. He'd asked her to leave town with him, but she didn't want to leave her sick mother. And he didn't have the heart to try to talk her into it at the time. Twelve years later when he heard her mother had died. He had thought of her and wanted to go see her. And find out if she still had any feelings for him. He never built up the nerve to do so. He did not want to feel those old emotions over again, if she rejected him once again.

Smiling Chase said, "Well beautiful of course I remember you, it isn't every day that you meet an angel".

Blushing Gail replied, "You always knew how to make a girl feel special…I'm sorry about what happened to your dad".

Grinning Chase responded, "Well he did what he did because he felt he had to, and he took ownership for doing it. Too bad it ended the way it did but there isn't no changing it now, so no sense trying to".

After a little more small talk Gail promised to stop back to see him, after he'd had some time to settle into the old place. He told her he looked forward to it, and not to be a stranger. So that answered that question. She did remember him. And if he was thinking straight, she still had at least some remaining feelings for him. Though he has to admit it had been twenty-five years since he had last been close to a female. As such he could be reading far more into things than were actually there.

Thinking to himself that being home might not be all that bad after all, he unlocked the door, fetched the crate from the floor; and then went inside his old…or rather new house. After depositing the crate onto the floor just inside the door, Chase closed and relocked the door.

He placed his head against the door, closed his eyes and thought. "What am I going to do with this place? I don't belong here anymore nor do I wanna move back to this shitty little town. Sure it would be fun to take up with Gail again, but she's likely involved…it's been a long, long time. And besides I've money enough now to go anywhere, and start over. Even more so if I do sell off the bar and the house. Not to mention anything else of value sitting around in them. Like these bottles of whisky."

The thought of starting fresh where no one knew him was very appealing. With a little more consideration he pushed off from the door thinking that was what he would do. Go through the house figure out what he would keep. Sell all the rest, and then sell the house too. So where to start?

Chase retrieved the crate from the floor and took it through to the kitchen, turning on lights as he moved further into the large house. Once in the kitchen he slid the crate onto a counter, and sat down at the table. As he mulled over his options, and he hand rolled a smoke, he decided to smoke it out on the back porch, out of respect for his father who had never smoked. He had never cared for the smell of them either.

Standing out on the creaky old porch he was hit with a wave of old memories. The more they came the more painful they became. Quickly tiring of the emotional assault from his past flooding back in, he pitched his half finished smoke into the dirt and went back inside. Looking through cupboards quickly revealed that there was very little food within the house. Figuring everything in town was closed he would have to make do with what little was in the place. As he was deciding what to make for supper, he heard a soft knock at the front door.

Chase opened the door to find Gail standing on the front porch with a wicker basket standing on the floor between her feet.

Blushing Gail said, "I'm sorry to bother you again tonight, but I got home and couldn't bear the thought of you sitting here all by yourself tonight. I made something for supper and figured I'd at least come over long enough to eat it with you. That is if you are in the mood for some company your first night back".

Laughing Chase replied, "I couldn't think of a better person to eat supper with. I was actually just trying to find something here to eat. Hopefully you won't get into hock with your husband for coming over here. Or for being gone to long if he is o.k. with you coming here in the first place".

Blushing even brighter Gail confessed, "Well that shouldn't be a problem as I'm not married. I haven't been with anyone since you moved away, to be perfectly honest with you. As much as that bothered my mother before she passed. She wanted to see me married off before she died. But truth be told, I missed you more and more with each passing day since you first left".

Chase was smiling like a mad fool, as he stepped aside and invited Gail inside. She bent down to pick up the basket, but Chase thought better of it and picked it up before she could.

Telling her, "The least I can do is carry the food, seeing as you went to all the trouble of making it and bringing it over here".

Gail smiled and stepped past him into the house saying, "I'd reserve your judgment on the food until after you've tasted it, and I'm not a very good cook".

Gail

Carrying the basket into the kitchen Chase told Gail to follow him and to make herself comfortable. Chase set the basket down on the table and began to search for some plates in the cupboards. He quickly found where they were and retrieved two for them to use. Not wanting to shorten his time with her, he decided to wash them before placing them on the table.

As he washed them they talked briefly about the past when they were kids. Gail removed items from the basket and placed them on the table leaving room for their plates. Chase was amazed by all the food she had packed into the basket. As he placed the plates on the table opposite each other he noted each item. There was a large cold roasted chicken, a medium round of cheese, some sliced apples, and pears, and four small loaves of fresh baked bread.

Smiling he said, "Damn girl, you trying to fatten me up or what? I haven't eaten this much food in one sitting in my entire life".

Gail blushed again and said, "I guess if the truth be known, I was a little nervous while packing the basket. I wasn't really thinking about what I was putting into it. I was just going through the motions and filled it up".

Laughing Chase said, "Well beautiful, what do you think should we raid my father's old wine cellar for something to wash all this food down with?"

Feeling like a little girl about to do something naughty Gail replied, "Sounds good to me, though I do believe it is now your wine to do with as you wish…Damn, sorry I didn't think".

Chase laughed long and hard before he could say, "No worries, I have to keep reminding myself that this old place is now mine. And everything inside it is too…well except for you. Let's go see what kind of wine we should have with supper".

Entering the dank dark basement Chase could tell that Gail was a little afraid. They quickly made their way over to the first shelf of bottles. Chase asked her what kind of wine she liked.

Gail said, "Well I've never really drank much wine so I don't know what's good and what isn't".

As Chase didn't know either, they quickly decided to just randomly grab a bottle each and leave it to chance. With wine in hand Gail led the way back up into the kitchen.

As they were walking back up the stairs Chase couldn't keep his eyes from admiring Gail's firm backside, as it swayed from side to side in her tight blue jeans.

Half way up the stairs Gail asked, "Liking what you see?"

As she looked back over her shoulder and, realized where he was looking.

Blushing like a fool Chase cleared his throat and said, "Ah, sorry about that…but ah yeah…you've always had a great looking bottom".

Back in the kitchen Chase busied himself with finding some glasses, and washing them. Giving him enough time for the heat; and color to drain from his face. As he worked he hoped to himself that the wine they picked out went well with the food Gail brought over.

They ate and drank the two bottles of wine, while talking about what they had been up to since they had last seen each other. Then they washed the dishes together and discussed what Chase's plans for the house and bar were. Once done they decided on sitting out on the front porch and drinking some more wine, while they talked. Chase moved two chairs out to the porch, and told Gail to sit and relax while he grabbed some more wine for them.

Chase quickly went back downstairs and grabbed the first four bottles he laid hands on then returned to the kitchen with them. He placed them all on the counter and opened one, before taking it out to the porch. He placed the remaining three in the refrigerator to chill them. He poured them both a glass before sitting down beside Gail. Over the next few hours they drank the four bottles of wine and talked about everything that entered their minds. When Gail stifled a yawn, Chase realized for the first time just how late it was. He offered to walk Gail back to her house.

Gail confessed to him that she was feeling a little tipsy, and asked him if it would be alright if she spent the night. Chase insisted that it was not a problem. The old house was more than big enough for the both of them. He excused himself to go figure out the sleeping arrangements, as he hadn't been upstairs yet. And didn't know where the beds were, or how many of them there actually were. The last time he had been in the house there had been five bedrooms upstairs. Though back then there were only three of them used as bedrooms. The other two had been used as storage rooms for one thing or another. He quickly found the beds and decided to remake two of the three. It had probably taken him longer than it should have to find the bed cloths. After what felt like an hour Chase had finished and walked back into the hall towards the stairs. Once back on the front porch Chase collected the empty glasses and bottles and returned them to the kitchen, then returned to Gail.

Taking her by the left hand Chase led Gail back inside the house and up the stairs. Chase showed her to one of the bedrooms, and then the other two. Confessing that he had only freshened up the beds in the first two rooms he'd shown her. Telling her she could take which ever bed she preferred and he'd take the other one. Gail chose the one in the second room; he had shown her merely because it was the room she was currently standing outside of. Chase left her there and told her he would see her in the morning. As a second thought he went into the room that had recently been his fathers. He chose a long sleeve button up shirt from the closet. Returning to the room he'd just left Gail in he knocked softly on the door.

Gail softly called out, "Come in I'm decent".

Chase opened the door with a sheepish grin spread across his face and said, "I thought you might like something to sleep in. This was one of my father's; it should serve you well as a night shirt".

Chase quickly walked into the room and set it gently on the end of the bed, then returned to the hallway.

Gail hadn't moved from the wash stand next to the shuttered window but replied, "Thank you, it will be perfect to sleep in".

Closing the door behind himself he went back downstairs to lock up for the night. While outside to fetch the chairs they had been sitting on, he sat down and rolled a smoke. Smoking it he went over the events of the night in his head. Smiling he pitched away the remainder of his smoke, and took the chairs back inside.

After locking up the front door he slowly climbed the stairs to go to bed. He walked slowly and as softly as he could as he did not want to disturb Gail in case she was already sleeping. After quickly using the washroom he headed for bed, in what used to be his father's room. Chase stripped off his cloths and climbed into the bed naked. Laying back with his eyes closed thinking of Gail sleeping in the next room in nothing but an old over sized shirt he felt his manhood growing hard. He drifted off to sleep with a smile on his face, with Gail still on his mind.

A few hours later Chase was awaken by a noise. Opening his eyes and listening to the dark, he tried to figure out what had awakened him; he heard the floor creak outside the bedroom door. In his half asleep state he didn't remember that Gail had slept over. After being alone for so many years he was not in the habit of thinking anyone was in the house with him, in the wee hours of the morning. He was about to reach for his gun hanging from the bed post when the door slowly opened. Chase froze in mid movement as he seen Gail's moon lit outline filling the doorway. As he took in the sight of her shapely body clearly outlined in the thin loose fabric, a flood of old memories washed over him. She looked even more beautiful standing there wearing nothing but his father's old button down shirt, then anything he could remember ever seeing her in. The moon clearly showcased her shapely figure through the thin material of the shirt, making him fall even more deeply in love with her. As he watched her slip into the room and close the door, he felt his manhood hardening for the second time of the night.

Within seconds Gail had crossed the floor and slid under the covers next to him.

When he moved over to give her some more room she said, "I hope I didn't wake you, I was cold and couldn't sleep very well in a strange bed. I hope you don't mind me joining you like this".

Chase smiled to himself hoping that she didn't realize his manhood was hard, and said in return, "Your welcome in my bed anytime the desire suits you".

Gail turned towards him, and pressed herself against him to give him a hug in thanks. Drawing a leg over his, her bare thigh lightly brushed his stiff member.

As her arm tightened around him she playfully said, "Sorry I didn't know you slept naked, but I do believe you're rather enjoying me being here with you more than your admitting".

Chuckling, Chase said, "oh really, and what makes you think that?"

Before he realized what she was going to do Gail's arm shifted to allow her hand to grasp his hard manhood, softly stroking it she said, "Well you're happy, I'm here, or this fella is acting on his own".

That was the end of the conversation for quite some time. They made love to each other for the next few hours, before falling asleep hold each other close. They both slept deeply until the late morning light spilling in the window woke them, by shinning in their eyes.

They made love one more time in the morning light before getting out of bed. Washing up and getting dressed; Chase confided in her that he was finding the notion of moving back permanently more and more appealing as time went by, largely due to her re-entering his life as she had. Laughing Gail told him she had some things she had to take care of before she was due at work. They made plans to meet back up for supper later in the evening. Chase walked Gail to the door, kissed her long and firmly. Wished her a good day at work before, watching her walk down the street, towards her house.

Chase went back inside to start his own work of going through the house, trying to figure out what he was going to do with everything. As he went into the kitchen to make himself a cup of coffee, he realized for the first time he didn't even know where Gail worked. He made a mental note to himself to ask her when she returned later that evening.

Chase decided that he would have a coffee and a smoke before getting started for the day. He had always enjoyed his first smoke and coffee of the day. Especially if he knew it was going to be a long tiring one. While the water was heating up on the old stove, Chase rolled a smoke and went out on the back porch to smoke it. As he smoked his thoughts wandered back to Gail and the night they had just spent together.

Finishing his smoke he returned to the brightly lit kitchen. He quickly made his coffee enjoying the heat from the bright morning sun beating through the dirty window over the sink and warming his side. With coffee in hand he wandered over to the table and sat down. His thoughts kept wandering back to Gail as he drank his coffee, enjoying the strong rich flavor of it. As he neared the end of the cup his thoughts shifted to the work ahead of him for the day.

As he finished drinking his coffee he decided to take a long hot bath before getting started. Once his bath was completed Chase rummaged around in his father's wardrobe for some old cloths to put on. He figured there was no sense in ruining his cloths as he rooted through the old house. He found an old faded pair of blue jeans and an ancient looking shirt and put them on. Sitting on the edge of the bed, Chase thought well I'm home.

Home

Chase figured starting at the top of the house and working his way down through the house was probably the best bet. He figured his father would have kept the more valuable things stored away down in the basement. That meant starting up in the attic. Chase went down the hall to the door at the far end of the house. He opened the door wide and looked into the mirror hanging from the inside of it, and wondered not for the first time, why he had come home.

He could have sold lock, stock, and barrel without ever entering his childhood home ever again. And it never would have bothered him. Then again, he knew his father had hoarded some very valuable things in the old house over the years. And he meant to find them if he could, before selling the place. Also there was the issue of Gail. Had he of not returned, last night never would have happened. And he would have missed out on an opportunity to rekindle their old flame. Only God knew where it would go from here. Though he hoped it would be a long lasting relationship. With any luck they would remain together for the remainder of their lives. Chase was ready to begin a long day of shifting through his new belongings. Figuring out what to keep and what to sell, or throw away. Chase thought his search could wait a little longer. He needed a coffee and a smoke, as the amount of work ahead of him sank in.

A short time later Chase was sitting on the back porch sipping hot black coffee, and smoking a hand rolled cigarette. It was going to be a hot sunny day. He was already sweating violently, and it would only get worse as the day grew older. Ten minutes later he figured he should get started before the old place got too hot, and sticky.

Chase headed into the small dank kitchen to put his cup in the sink for later. He'd wash it once there were enough dirty dishes to make it worth his while. As he turned to leave the kitchen, he heard something topple over down in the basement. Cursing loudly to himself, he decided he had better check it out. Knowing it was likely just a mouse or a rat. But that he should get rid of it before it destroyed everything of value in the basement.

Opening the basement door, Chase reached in and turned on the light. Something went skittering across the floor into the shadows, at the bottom of the stairs. Chase couldn't see what it was, but it didn't sound very big. Grabbing an old broken broom handle as he passed it, Chase descended the rickety old age worn stairs. Chase had to pause at the bottom of the stairs to allow his eyes to adjust to the dim light within the basement. He could see there were a lot of shadowy area's but not much else. After a couple of minutes Chase figured he could see as well as he ever was going to without additional light sources.

Looking around the large open area without moving from the bottom of the stairs, Chase saw a fair number of shelving units scattered around the room. Some over crowded with boxes, most over packed with bottles lying on their sides. He assumed this was the bulk of his late father's private wine collection. And still a few more shelving units here and there had hardly anything on them. All in all it reminded him of the small warehouse at the mill.

Against the furthest wall from him was a long work bench. There looked to be a large amount of things piled haphazardly on it. Or it could be covered with a bunch of large things. The light within the room was not good enough to tell for sure from where he was standing. Chase could also tell from where he was standing that majority of the open space under the work bench had been filled in with stuff also. Sitting across the room on top of an old barrel, Chase could clearly see a large fat grey rat sitting openly in a fat beam of light. Staring at Chase; as if he had no business being in the basement as it was his domain. The rat looked to be about the same size of a medium sized cat.

Chase drew the gun he always wore on his left hand hip, drew a bead, and fired a single shot at the rat. His aim was true and the rat flipped backwards off the barrel. Chase waited patiently for the ringing in his ears to fade, before heading further into his late father's private sanctum to collect his trophy. Smiling to himself as he crossed the room he wondered if he had been a gun slinger in a previous life. As the feel of the cold hard iron in his hand, felt too natural for his limited experience with it.

Chase found the dead rat lying on its side against a dust covered old chest of some sort. As Chase bent down to retrieve the rat, he realized that his bullet had obliterated the rat from its fuzzy little shoulders on up. As he grabbed it's now stiffening tail hauling it up, a stray ray of light reflected off the old trunk and caught his eye. As he left the basement with the rat, he decided to come back and check out the chest first before heading up into the top of the house.

Chase exited the house through the back door off the kitchen and tossed the dead rat into a battered old trash barrel. Chuckling to himself, he thought, my aim was true. I did not forget the face of my father. He remembered seeing an oil lamp on a shelf in his father's library and decided to fetch it before going back down into the dingy basement. Chase stopped in the kitchen to rummage through the drawers, looking for some matches.

His effort was rewarded when he found a small box with three matches inside it. It took all three matches to light the lamp. As the first two sputtered out as quickly as they flared to life. With the lit lamp in his hand he descended the old stairs back down into the basement.

Setting the lamp on the floor beside the old chest, Chase knelt in front of the chest and hauled it out from under the bench. It was surprisingly heavy, for so small a chest. Once in the light Chase realized for the first time that the chest was very, very old. It had strange looking carvings all over the top and sides. Chase decided to take it back upstairs with him where he could see it better.

Chase looked for handles to make it easier to carry, however he quickly discovered there weren't any. After a couple of failed attempts Chase finally had the heavy old chest up in the air. It was a long slow walk back to the stairs. He had to stop three times to set the chest down and rest, it was that heavy. Once at the bottom of the stairs he decided the best way to get the chest loaded with god knows what up them, was to lift it one step at a time. It would take him a hell of a long time doing it that way. However that way he could rest as he needed to and not have to worry about losing his balance and either dropping and damaging it, or falling down the stairs with it.

After what seemed like an hour Chase reached the kitchen. His back ached like a sore tooth. He was covered in sweat and old dust. He decided to take a short rest to regain some strength, and to muster the resolve he would need to boost the chest up into the air once more. A long while later, with a mighty heave Chase hoisted the chest back up into the air once more and slowly walked across the room. Chase placed the chest down on the bare table, so it would be easier to see, and work with.

With the bright overhead light shining down on the dirty old chest, coupled with the strong sunlight spilling in through the kitchen windows, Chase leaned against the counter to take a better look at the hidden treasure he had found. The chest was approximately two and a half feet long, two feet wide, and two and a half feet deep. The top and all four sides were covered in what looked to be hand carved panels of some old darkly colored wood. With insets of what appeared to be either silver or gold. Thought the chest was so covered with dust that it was still impossible to tell what the carvings were of, or what the metal actually was. Or for that matter if it were even metal, and not just some trick of the light.

After a short hunt under the sink Chase found a few old rags. Wetting them to make the job easier, he set to work at cleaning the chest off. It took him well over an hour to clear all of the dust off of the chest; it was so thick and caked on. By the time he was finished he was streaked with dirt all the way up to his elbows and most of his face from where he continuously wiped away his sweat. There had to be at least sixty years of dust caked to the chest, if not more.

Laughing, as he walked over to the sink to wash some of the dirt off himself, he thought, "I'm going to get wrinkled hands after having them in water so much".

He figured he had rinsed out his rags at least fifty times in the process of cleaning the chest off. Though once clean the chest shimmered in the strong overhead light. It looked to be made from a single piece of mahogany or black cherry. And the metal turned out to be gold, set into the wood in numerous places to help accent what could only be a hand carved scene. Chase bent closer to peer at the carvings and detected a faint aroma of cherry. So it was made from black cherry after all, which meant that the chest had to be worth a fortune.

The carvings were beautiful and very well done. They almost looked real enough to get up off the chest and move around they were that good and life like. There were carvings of trees, old looking houses, and beautiful looking women covering each surface. There was also an ancient looking lock attached to what appeared to be the front of the chest, by a solid gold clasp. Though he couldn't identify any hinges on what he figured to be the back of the chest. Nor for that matter a break in the carved scene's identifying a lid.

The lock was too sturdy to easily break (not that he wanted to as it also looked very valuable). It also appeared to be made of solid gold. The lock had also been finely carved and depicted a forest scene. And he doubted that he possessed the skills needed to easily pick the lock, to open it. There was also a very strong risk of damaging the chest if he wasn't careful enough or slipped up even slightly. The only safe method to open the lock would be to find the key for it. But if his father owned the key for the lock where the hell would it be, seeing as he said he never had it. Or at least not that he had ever been aware of. It could have been easily left in the house along with the chest by its previous owner. Then again it could just have easily have been lost centuries ago.

Looking closer at the panels covering the chest, in an attempt to understand some meaning to them, Chase found a small rectangle slightly bigger than the tip of his thumb on what he thought of as the bottom rear panel. That didn't really fit in with the rest of the panel. Baffled that after spending so much time to painstakingly carve out each panel, why the craftsman would allow for this one little flaw. Chase traced the area with a fingertip, as he contemplated it.

He heard a slight shifting sound emitting from the area, and the small rectangle popped open revealing a hidden compartment. Carefully pulling on the little piece of wood Chase pulled it free from the chest. It was also surprisingly heavy for its size. Turning it over in his hands as he looked closer at it Chase realized it was actually a little slide top box. The contents of it were likely what gave it its unusual weight. The little box also sported the same type of hand carved scene as the chest did. There was no doubt that it was an original part of the chest, and not a later addition.

Chase slowly slide the box open. Inside was a single key. It looked as old as the lock that was fastened to the front of the chest. It was very heavy and also looked to be made of solid gold. Carefully Chase put the end you'd hold onto while using the key into his mouth and bit down on it. He could feel his teeth slowly sinking into the soft metal. Yup it was solid gold.

The key had to be worth thousands of dollars by itself. Never mind the lock or the chest themselves. Or for that matter whatever was hidden inside the chest. Chase figured he might as well try opening the lock with the key, even though his instincts screamed at him that he would ruin the key. As he figured that the key was too weak to be used as a real key, being made from solid gold. To his ultimate surprise the lock easily opened with the slightest bit of pressure he applied to the key. It was almost as if the lock was brand new, or used frequently.

With a shaking hand Chase removed the freshly sprung lock from the chest and set it gently off to the left of the chest on the table on top of a dry rag. Holding his breath Chase slowly twisted the now free clasp open and lifted up on the top of the chest. To his surprise the top of the chest swung silently upward in his hands, revealing a hidden hinge running the full length of the back of the chest. It also looked to be made of solid gold. He was so surprised by what he found inside that he sank down into a chair and laughed like a fool for at least five minutes.

Wiping the tears that were still spilling from his eyes away, Chase reached into the chest and pulled out an ancient looking book. The book was slightly longer than his hand and just as wide. It was about two fingers thick and bound in what looked like three hundred year old leather. It was so black and dry, it looked like it would turn into ash were he to open the book.

Turning it over to look closer at each side of the book, Chase soon realized there was nothing on the outside of it. With no marking on the outside he had no choice but to try opening it to find out what it was. Being as careful as he possibly could he slowly opened the book. The books covering held together just fine. It was actually in great shape, with no cracks or tears or imperfections in it what so ever. The pages inside the book were of a thick material that didn't feel like paper. To be perfectly honest with himself, the thought of dried skin floated across Chase's mind's eye. Chase soon realized that because of the unusual thickness of the pages. There were actually very few pages in it. There might be two dozen of them in total, or not many more than that.

But that was just a crazy thought. "No one would fashion a book out of dried human skin…would they? No, no of course not. What was he thinking so morbidly like that for? That was just nuts…wasn't it?"

But the words in the book looked like they were in the material not on it. Was it actually dried skin that had been tattooed, and then made into a book? Chase laughed at himself for his foolishness. But then again anything was possible really. And besides what did it really matter. He could easily destroy the book and no one would ever know it even existed. Let alone that he now owned it. It was definitely old and dry enough to easily catch fire and burn quickly.

He set it aside and decided to attempt to read it later. As he was still not convinced that it wouldn't fall apart in his hands once he began to turn more and more pages as he read it.

As he reached into the chest to retrieve the next item he thought to himself with a chuckle, "The book looks a little dry".

Before his hand was able to close over the next item in the chest, Chase heard a knock on his front door. Cursing to himself he replaced the book in the chest. Closed it and refastened the lock on the front of it. Taking the extra time he replaced the key in the slide top box and put it back into its place. Leaving the chest on the table top he went to answer the door.

Half way to the front door he thought better of leaving the valuable chest out in open view.

Stopping he yelled out, "Just a minute".

Turned and quickly returned to the kitchen. When he had been looking for the matches earlier he had found a drawer full of table cloths. He went to that drawer and got one out. Unfolding it part of the way he draped it over the chest, hiding it from sight. Once he was satisfied that it was completely covered he left the kitchen, and answered the door.

Standing just outside the door when he opened it was Gail. She was wearing a long dress with a tight high collar held in place under her chin, with a cameo pin. Chase ushered her into the house, smiling to himself, as a flash back of the night before hit him. Gail led the way into the kitchen. As they drew closer to the kitchen Gail noticed the large covered item on the table for the first time.

Stopping she turned back towards Chase and said, "Did I call at a bad time?"

Smiling Chase assured her that she was more than welcome to stop by anytime she wanted to.

Chase slipped past her and stood in the doorway, effectively blocking her from the kitchen, before asking, "Would you like to see what I had found down in the basement?"

When she told Chase that she would he told her to close her eyes.

When she had them firmly closed Chase went to the table and removed the tablecloth from the top of the chest, then said, "Ok, you can open your eyes now".

Opening her eyes Gail looked at what Chase had uncovered as she began to walk again. She stopped just inside the kitchen with her bottom jaw resting on her chest.

Quickly pulling herself together she exclaimed, "That is the most beautiful chest I've ever seen. Where did it come from? It must have cost a fortune".

Laughing Chase confessed, "I hear a noise in the basement. I went down seen a big rat, and shot it. When I collected the body, I saw the chest. It was covered in years of dirt and dust. I brought it up here and cleaned it off. That was underneath all the layers".

Gail went over to it and spent a long time silently looking it over.

When she was finished she said, "Even that old beautiful lock looks expensive. Did you find a key for it too?"

Laughing Chase said, "Look at the chest a little closer, it hold a little secret I don't think you've seen yet".

Gail spent the next hour looking over the chest in silent determination, trying to find the "little secret" Chase had mentioned to her.

Finally she gave up and said, "I think I'll be able to see those flawless carvings in my sleep. But I didn't find the "little secret" you were talking about"

With a knowing grin Chase walked over to the table. Took Gail by the hand and lead her around the table to the back of the chest.

He pointed out the little rectangle he'd found earlier to her and said, "run your finger tip around that little rectangle and see what happens".

Thinking Chase was poking fun at her, she reluctantly did as he told her and traced the little rectangle.

When she was finished tracing it she heard a sliding sound coming from it and jumped back.

When the little rectangle popped out she laughed at herself and said, "Well isn't that just neat, I never would have noticed it if you didn't show me. How did you find it?"

Chase confessed that he merely noticed the seemingly unrelated area and was running his finger over it absently, when it popped open for him. Chase allowed her to pull the little box free and discover what it was for herself. When she had the heavy key in hand she asked him if it was really gold. He confessed that it was. Then he told her that it even opened the lock, very easily and told her to give it a try. Gail opened the lock with the slightest turn of the key. After a quick glance at Chase she removed the lock and placed it on the cloth to the left of the chest. Unbeknown to her in the exact same place Chase had placed it, when he had removed it.

When she hesitated Chase said, "Go ahead and open it, I already have. It is perfectly safe to do so. There is nothing inside that can hurt you, well I guess unless you let it".

Gail twisted the clasp open and slowly lifted the lid of the chest. With more than a little fear in her heart, she stepped closer a step and peered inside. Smiling she lifted out the ancient looking book. She placed it on the table on the opposite side from the lock, not wanting to damage it. Then looked back inside the chest to see what else was in it.

Laughing she said, "Isn't that fitting, more bottles of wine. I should have guessed".

Chase laughed and said in return, "Yeah I thought the same thing when I opened it just before you came. I think if my father had been able to open the chest, he might have thought the same thing".

Smiling, Gail asked, "So what are you going to do with them?"

Chase replied, "Well I've been thinking about that as I was watching you look at and open the chest. And I've decided I'll drink a bottle or two, and likely either sell the others or add them to my father's collection".

As he spoke he reached into the chest and pulled out a couple of bottles, and placed them on the table next to the lock. He confessed to Gail that he was curious about what was in the old book. He told her that he planned on sitting down with a glass of wine, and reading it.

Gail told him, "I think I drank more than enough wine last night to do me for a few days. I think I'll leave you to it and call it a night".

She looked into Chase's eyes with a playful smile spreading across her face, and a twinkle in her eyes. Chase thought that he would enjoy a quiet night to himself to study his recent find.

To Gail he said, "Well I have to admit I drank more wine last night than I ever have in the past. Though I love your company, I would like to find out what secrets that book holds".

Gail said to him, "Well then it is final, I'll go home and leave you to it. I'll stop back over tomorrow night after work. You'd best be ready for me then, because I'll be bringing some supper with me. And I'll be looking for some desert after that".

Chase hoped that she was referring to sex, because he was looking forward to getting her back into bed too. They briefly kissed good night in the kitchen, before Chase walked her to the door. When she had reached the edge of his yard, he reentered the house and locked it up for the night. Not expecting anyone else to stop by.

As he headed back to the kitchen he turned off all the other lights as he went. He hoped that by doing so, if anyone else decided to stop by they'd think he wasn't home. Not that he could imagine anyone else coming to his door. Chase sat back down at the table and looked over the carved panels on the chest once more. Before he knew he'd picked it up, in his hand was a dusty old bottle. Cleaning it off with a damp rag that was handy he read the label.

There were two words hand written on it in fancy lettering. After a couple of minutes he made out the words. The label read, "Immortal Wine". Turning the bottle around and around in his hand Chase admired the fancy lettering on the label and how it glinted in the overhead light. It looked like the lettering on the label was done in gold. They must have been expensive bottles of wine when they were placed in the chest, judging by the labels and the sealed neck. Immortal Wine…so his assumptions were right, it was wine in the bottles. Likely hundreds of years old by the looks of them and knowing his father, the old fool never would have guessed they were inside the chest at all.

The top of the bottle was sealed in bright red wax covering what appeared looking through the bottle neck to be a cork. Other than the dirty old looking label the bottle was plain dark green glass. Inside the chest there were four more bottles and nothing else.

Chase set the bottle off to the side of the chest with the other one he'd taken out before, and thought, "Well after the morning I've had I think I deserve to at least try the wine. After all I've five more bottles to sell. I can drink one".

He rummaged around the kitchen until he found a cork screw and a glass, and then returned to the table.

Immortal Wine

With his old pocket knife Chase first scored then removed the old wax seal from the bottle, as his father had taught him to do countless years before. With slow long practiced skill Chase applied the cork screw and removed the cork from the bottle. Setting it aside he left the bottle on the table to "air" also as he father had taught him to do with a fine bottle of wine. As it "aired" he went out onto the back porch for a hand rolled cigarette.

As he leaned against the railing smoking he thought of everything his father had taught him about wine over the long forgotten years of his youth. He knew that the longer a wine aged the mellower it would be. Providing it had been stored properly. Otherwise it would be rendered into vinegar, and be worthless. Well the dusty damp old basement was definitely the perfect environment to store and age fine wine.

He just hoped that it had been as well stored before it came into his father's possession. Pitching his butt across the rail into the dusty yard Chase re-entered the kitchen. Sitting back down at the table Chase picked up the bottle of wine and sniffed it to determine if it was wine or vinegar. It smelled of strawberries, blueberries and currents, but not vinegar.

Considering himself fortunate Chase poured a small amount of the dark liquid from the bottle into his waiting glass. Spinning it around the glass while he held it up to the light (also as his father had taught him to do) Chase could see through the dark red liquid and see that it was crystal clear with nothing floating in it. He took a small hesitant sip of it. Fully prepared to spit it back out if it tasted foul.

The wine immediately made his mouth water for more. It was cool from the temperature in the basement. It was smooth as silk in his mouth and as it trickled down his throat. It was slightly sweet and held a pleasant after taste. All in all it was an excellent wine. And that was saying volumes as Chase had never been one to truly enjoy any wine.

Chase tipped up his glass and quickly finished off the wonderful liquid inside it. Then filled the glass to the top, and with bottle still in hand promptly drained almost the entire glass. Before refilling it again and setting the bottle back down. He decided that he had better slowly sip it from then on as he didn't know the alcohol content or what effects it would have on him. After one more, long sip he decided that by reading the book that had come in the chest with the wine, he'd be more apt to drink the wonderful liquid slower.

Before he actually picked up and opened the book again. Chase emptied and refilled his glass once more. To his pleasant surprise he wasn't feeling the usual effects liquor produced in him. He actually felt wide awake, full of vigor, and unbelievably thirsty. Chase studied the book a little more as he continued to sip his wine. He was just about to start reading it when he realized his glass was empty, and so was the bottle.

With a grunt of irritation he quickly opened a second bottle and refilled his glass, then began to read the book. On the first page was a short note, which read:

Dear, whoever you are...

If you are reading this then you have managed to open my little box of immortality. And YES I DO

Immortal Wine

MEAN IMMORTALITY. For with this book you will have found six bottles of MY Immortal Wine. This is a very, very special wine, and should NOT be drunk until this book has been read from cover to cover.

With a short laugh Chase thought, "Well dear book, I'm a little ahead of you there".

As he picked up his glass, saluted the book with it and then took a long drink from it. He placed his glass defiantly back on the table and kept reading.

Providing you have not reversed the intended order of things and ARE READING THIS BOOK FIRST, you still have a choice. If you have already DRANK even a drop of MY wine, it is already too late to undo what has been done!

But I hope I'm not getting ahead of myself, as I sometimes do. As I was saying this is a very, very special wine. It was originally made and bottled in 1801 deep in some mountains that have no current name. In a little village I found by chance. I enjoyed the wine so much that I decided to use this wine as the base of MY very special wine. I bought six bottles of the wine with the promise not to kill everyone in the little village.

And this was no little promise on my part... TRUST ME ON THIS... but I'm getting ahead of myself again, please forgive me.

I mixed a very special ingredient into each of the bottles of wine before resealing them. Then storing them into the chest

49

you discovered them in. The chest is of no real importance. I acquired it one day while wandering through a dark part of middle Europe sometime between 1792 and 1795. Whereas it is considerably older than the wine, it is hardly of value at all in comparison to MY wine. If you wish to learn what makes my wine so special, and the box valueless in comparison to it read on and learn what you should know before drinking it. Again I hope your reading first, then drinking...and not the other way around. But if not... I say simply WELCOME!

Chase thought this was a rather cryptic message indeed. Draining his glass, and refilling once more Chase read on.

I have prepared you as best as I can, and can only hope it is not too late... therefore I will continue on with my sorted little tale. Enjoy, the knowledge...

Chase flipped past a couple of blank pages, before coming across more writing. He managed to finish the second bottle of wine getting to this point. He decided that he would not drink anymore before finding out what all the cryptic messages were about. He placed the now empty bottles back inside the chest, and relocked it. Then, he went through the process of returning the key to its original place. Chase figured that by going to this length he would help ensure that he would not be drinking anymore of the wine. As a further precaution to ensure he simply would not get into the chest once more tonight, he opened two bottles of wine from a basement shelf. With this task done Chase picked up the book and wine before going upstairs to his bedroom.

Immortal Wine

After stripping down the covers and crawling into bed. Chase propped himself up on some spare pillows and got comfortable, before resuming reading.

My name at this point in time (not that it even matters) is Vladimir Von Vanpier. I was born in the year 1442, in a little Scandinavian village. My family was well off and, I had to wish for nothing. I grew to be a fine looking young man. Though self admittingly I was a spoiled rotten braggart and a scamp. If I wanted something I took it. If I wanted someone they were mine. I didn't think in terms of right or wrong. Only in terms of mine or I want it.

I would make items mine or even ladies if I desired them. Though I was rash and brutish I never was what you'd call a ladies' man. I was cruel and violent with my women suitors and was constantly alone as a result of it. Though I was of marrying age my family was beside themselves wondering if I'd ever settle down and get married. I alone knew the truth of the matter.

One night while drinking with a lady I picked up at a ball, we were walking alone along a forest path when the moonlight spilled through the trees, across the tops of her breasts. As they spilled from the top of her low cut ball gown. I instantly had to have her. I pulled her into the forest and ripped her clothing from her terrified body. When I had her naked I beat her savagely and raped her multiple times.

Reading this confession Chase's stomach began to turn, however he continued to read on, compelled to find out the outcome, and what other information the book held in store for him.

When I was finished with her I slit her throat and left her under a small pile of dead leaves next to a fallen log. Then I redressed myself and re-found the path. I only made it a couple of yards from where I left the poor girl, when I was overcome and pulled into the woods myself. I was attacked, robed and left for dead. Obviously I did not die...well sort of.

I don't know how much time had passed, whether it had been minutes, hours or days. All I knew was when I came back to my senses I'd been profoundly changed. Everything was in sharper focus; I could see every detail of every object around me. I could hear and smell and see like never before. Hell I even knew I could close my eyes and walk back to the exact spot I'd left my misfortunate mistress.

It was very dark, though I could see as clearly as if it were the middle of the day. I felt strong and alive despite having been attacked and severely beaten. There was only one thing I could sense as being amiss. I was extremely thirsty. I felt like I could drink an entire river dry. Though I suppose that really wasn't that surprising given that I couldn't remember the last time I had something to drink, nor how long I had been left for dead after my horrific beating. I walked back into the little village, and found a small watering hole that was open at that time of night. It must have been quite late for it was the only place I could find that was still open.

I swung open the door and walked inside. There were but a few people left inside. I could smell stale beer, mead, and cheap rotgut. As well as all the odors wafting off of the handful of people around the room, I found a small table in a dark corner and sat down. I was in no mood to be pestered, nor stared at by my bar mates.

Within a few minutes, a pretty little red headed girl came slowly over to my table, bending at the waist to afford me with the best possible view of her perky firm little breasts. As her loose fitting top fell easily open to afford a view of every inch, smiling she asked me what she could get me, clearly indicating that even she was on the menu if I liked. I ordered a stein of mead, and some company once I'd had a couple more to drink. I don't know if she detected the change I felt within myself, or if something else made her jerk back from the table and hurry away towards the bar without a further word, or backwards glance. Or if my slight smile was somehow off to her. It certainly felt strange to me and nothing like my usual smile.

I ran a hand over my face as I considered the drastic sudden change in the girl. Only to pull it quickly back in fright. It had to be my imagination. There was no other rational explanation I could think of. However I was positive that two of my front top teeth were now protruding *out of my mouth and slightly over my lower lip. But again I am getting ahead of myself. And besides I believe I've given you enough to digest so far. I suggest that you stop reading here and take some time to consider what I have said so far. Then if you still want to know more come on back to my little book, and pick up where you left off.*

Though before you close these covers, for the time being I'll leave you with one last thought. DO YOU WANT TO BE IMMORTAL? If you truthfully answered YES, drink some of MY wine. If not you had best leave it alone!

Chase closed the book and laid it on the top of the bedside table. Shaking his head to try to clear it of the cryptic writing he'd just read. Either the author of that book was a lunatic, or was truly mad. There was little in the book that made sense. And Chase doubted that his reading more of it would benefit him any. However looking at his pocket watch he realized it was after four in the morning. Even though he didn't feel tired, he decided he should try to get some sleep. No matter how hard or what he tried to think about that strange little book occupied his mind entirely. When he could no longer resist the urge he picked the book back up and flipped it open again, no longer afraid to damage it, for the first time since he laid his eyes on it.

Chase quickly found the spot where he has stopped reading. Turning past the page in anticipation of what other secrets the book would reveal; Chase was deflated when he discovered the next page was blank, as well as the next page and the next. He was beginning to get upset as he turned more and more pages only to find the remainder of the book was blank. Yup he told himself it would figure. Only he could find a book written by a lunatic. And the son of a bitch had only written enough in it to draw him in and want more.

Upset at how the book had ended, and of the fool it had made of him. Chase tossed the book down on the small table beside the bed. He then went to the washroom before returning to the bedroom, and stripped off his dirty cloths. Knowing the sun would be coming up soon, and not wanting it to wake him as he planned on sleeping in. Chase drew the heavy dark curtains closed to help keep out the coming light. He laid down on the bed and fell asleep almost at once.

Awakening

Chase slept like the dead for the first time in many years. He didn't stir or dream the entire time he was asleep. At least not that he could remember. When he crawled out of bed he felt strange. He couldn't remember the last time he had felt so refreshed and recharged after a night's sleep. His senses seemed to be sharper. Though it was dark in the room he could make out every detail of everything inside the bedroom. He could also hear things that he never noticed before. Come to think of it, he could even smell things he never noticed in the past. For the first time in a long, long time he was scared. Maybe there was something to all that crap he had read in that strange book.

Chase reached for his pocket watch to see what time it was. His movements were faster than they had right to be. It seemed like he merely thought about picking his watch up and it was in his hand. Shaking his head in disbelief he pressed the button to open the cover. To his astonishment the watch crumbled in his hand. With a start Chase wondered what the hell was going on. He seemed to be stronger, faster, and for lack of better words, better than he had ever been. Immortality nothing…that wine if that was the cause, had made him a new man.

Chase took his time to wash up and dress. Once he had finished and was sitting at his kitchen table once more. It seemed to him that the whole process had only taken him about five seconds. But now he was thinking crazy. There was no way on earth that he could have moved that fast. As crazy as it now seemed to him, Chase picked up the book once more to see if it held any information that would be helpful to him. Opening the book Chase couldn't believe his eyes. Everything he had read the night before was gone. He quickly closed the book and looked over the outside. It looked to be the same book. As he was already sure it was. He had brought it back downstairs with him, when he came down. And it was exactly where he had left it the night before. Besides if someone had entered his room last night, he would have woken up.

Opening it up again he looked over the first few pages. They were still blank. That wasn't possible. There definitely was writing on them last night. Not believing his eyes, Chase dropped the book back onto the table. He quickly got up and checked all the doors and windows, to see if anything had been left unlocked. Confirming everything was still locked up tight. So no one could have switched the book, for one that looked the same, as he already knew. He returned to the kitchen to see if he could determine what had happened to the book since he had slept.

Chase opened the book one final time. He slowly flipped through all the pages. All were blank with the exception of a short entry on the very last page. There were only a few lines, which read:

SO YOU DECIDED TO DRINK MY WINE! WELCOME TO IMMORTALITY. THIS BOOK WILL BE OF NO FURTHER USE TO YOU AS YOUR EYES CAN NO LONGER SEE THE OTHER INK. LOOK A LITTLE CLOSER AT MY CHEST, WITH YOUR NEW EYES... AND ENJOY YOUR REVELATIONS!

Alrighty, so what the hell was that suppose to mean? With my new eyes look over the chest again. What the hell he'd already spend hours looking it over and finding its secrets. Well the book couldn't help him anymore, so he might as well follow its cryptic final message. Chase closed the book and laid it down on the table to the right of the chest. Then he stood up to look over the chest from all sides once more, with his "NEW EYES".

Chase spent what felt like hours looking back over the chest. However judging by the suns path along the floor it could have only been mere minutes. The only new detail that he could see that he didn't before was that a pair of eyes on one of the carved women, looked to be make of separate pieces of gold. He put the tips of a finger against each eye. He pulled them back quickly as he felt them shift under his touch. He had to wonder how many other secrets the chest could hold.

To Chase's astonishment he heard a loud click as he touched the eye's just before jerking his hand back a hidden drawer slide open in the bottom of the chest. The drawer was only about as deep as one of his fingers was wide. It slid out about half an inch before stopping. Chase carefully eased the drawer slowly open. Inside was a small pile of loose paper. Chase reached into the drawer and pull out the small stack of paper. The paper was just as thick as the paper in the book. It looked to be made of the same type of material as that in the book.

Chase thumbed through the pages. The writing appeared to be from the same hand that had written the book. At this point in time he figured he had nothing to lose, so he might as well read the few pages. Maybe they would help him figure out what was going on. But before he got into reading it he needed a smoke to help him calm down. As he walked to the front door he rolled himself a cigarette. Opening the front door he saw an envelope on the porch with his name on it. Wondering what it could be he bent down and picked it up. He walked across the porch and laid it on the railing. Once his cigarette was lit he picked it back up and opened it. It was a letter from Gail. Leaning against the railing he read.

Dearest Chase,

I would have thought that after the night we spent together. You might have had the dignity to at least tell me you weren't interested in me. You didn't have to disappear back out of my life again. I am a grown woman and can handle rejection. It has been three day's since I last seen or heard from you. I'm secure enough to admit that you have constantly been on my mine since I first ran into you, when you returned to town. I would like to think that I have at least entered your mind in the past three days.

Even if you are not at all interested in a long term relationship with me, or a short term one for that matter. I deserve to at least hear it from you. I never would have expected you to just shut me out completely and ignore me. Now I feel used, angry, and hurt. I guess I have more feelings for you than you have for me. I do not regret finding my way to your bed our last and only night together. Nor making love to you until the early hours of the morning. Or the final coupling we had in the morning after we woke up.

I figured I would leave this note for you at your house. Where I have no idea if you are still in town or not. I really hope that you are. And the only reason I haven't seen or heard from you, is because you are afraid were moving too fast into a relationship. But I doubt I will ever find out the reason, as frankly at this point I don't expect to ever see you again.

If you change your mind and would like to see me again you know where I live. I haven't moved from my childhood home. I will understand either way. Though I do hope you will at least come to me and say goodbye, if you haven't already moved on. If the truth be known as it should, I fell back in love with you when I saw you'd returned. And a part of me hoped you had too. Hoping to hear from you, ...soon.

With all my heart,
Gail

What the hell...three day's there is no way it had been three days. He had just seen Gail last night...didn't he? Something strange definitely was going on here. It isn't possible that he had been asleep for three whole days. He was going to have to go over to Gail's and straighten everything out. There was no other way around it. But if what she said was true and it had been three day's since he'd last seen her, how was he going to explain that?

He figured he had better go back to his kitchen and read the pages. It wouldn't be very good if Gail was passing by and found him lounging on the front porch reading, if she thought he was ignoring her. He picked the loose pages up off the railing and went back inside. He stopped and locked the front door before heading back into the kitchen. Once he made himself a cup of coffee, he sat back down at the table to read the pages.

Welcome back... I see you have found the little secret I told you to look for...good!

So you have decided to drink my special wine, congratulations. However your life can no longer be what it once was. For you are no longer like the people around you. You see better, smell better, hear better, are faster, stronger, and will outlive them all. You are now a full-fledged vampir, as we are known in most parts of the world. The English call us Vampire's. However we are known by many different names around the world. It is enough to say you are now a drinker of blood.

No one but another vampire is truly safe around you. Mortal blood will call to you. Don't believe me? Try closing your eyes and listen. What do you hear? ... I know you can hear the ebb and flow of blood in the humans around you. Depending on how close they are to you, how loud the sound will be. Even the animals around you are not safe from your detection. Whereas their life blood flows at a different rhythm from humans, you can still detect it.

And believe you me, sometimes you will have to rely on it. Though for the best results of curbing your hunger, human blood is always best. Other blood will work, but you have to drink a great deal more of it to sustain yourself. That being said, you will have to feed soon. As a newly awakened fledg-

ling you need to feed or you will go into a blood lust. Trust me you don't want that to happen. If it does anyone could die at your hands and you would never know it until it was too late.

Might I suggest that you find some low-life that all villages, towns, cities, and hamlets seem to have a multitude of to feed upon; that way you can drink your fill, and not have to worry about anyone missing them. Take special care not to draw attention to yourself. Either dispose of the body by making it look like it's a victim of a crime, or put it where it won't be found for a long time. Either way, don't just leave it to be found. You are now able to live for centuries, but you can still die.

Albeit you are very close to impossible to kill. You need to be careful around fire. Were we do not need it for any warmth; it is pleasant to be around sometimes. Just as it can be used to help you blend in among mortals, especially on cold nights. It is often a safe bet that if mortals have a fire going in their homes, you should too. You are not fire proof; as such it can destroy you. Having your head removed from your body will also kill you. Other than that, no matter what you might have heard about vampires, or think you know about them (US). We are virtually indestructible.

Just as no two people are the same. The same holds true for vampires as well. Some of us need to feed more often than others. Some are stronger than others. Some are faster than others...etc...etc...etc... You will figure all this out on your own, providing you live long enough to learn these things. All you really need to know, to enable you to survive at this point. I've already told you. You must eat, and cover your tracks. Don't draw attention to yourself. Regardless of the century you're living in, people still fear us. We are the things that go bump in the night. And likely always will be hunted as a result of it.

Depending on how well you learn and blend in, will dictate how long you will live. There are very few reasons why you couldn't live forever. Also it is fair to warn you there are other creatures around the world that are long lived like we are. Over the course of time you will likely run into daemons (or demons if you prefer), and witches. They are the most common creatures at this time besides others like us, though they are definitely not the only ones. For the most part, you will have to travel to some extremely remote places to encounter some of the others.

However I will leave them for you to discover on your own. ...Or not. The only other pieces of must know information I should share with you at this point are; you don't need to sleep...ever...however if you desire to lay down and fall asleep remember, time moves differently for us while we sleep as it does while we are awake. What might feel like only a few minutes could in reality be hours, days, months or even years! Therefore it is of the utmost importance to choose your sleeping place carefully. You don't want some human finding you while you are asleep and virtually defenseless.

Daylight does not hurt us. No matter what you might have heard. We do not burn to a crisp in the sunlight, or other fables that humans like to tell each other. You can eat human food if you want to try to fit in. However do not gorge yourself on it, as it can make you physically sick, and cause you to vomit. As I said before these are only the basics that you need to know. If you want to know more come and find me. I will answer all your questions for you if you do decide to seek me out.

The chest in front of you has one more little secret to it. Take the time to remove all of the bottles and then the packaging materials surrounding them. You will find a map inset into the bottom of the chest. Study the map well. Then come and see me. I do not venture far anymore. As such will be where the map indicates that I will be. You do not need to bring the chest nor map with you. As with many other traits, your memory has been seriously enhanced with your vampiric blood. If you take the time to study it well, you will never ever forget what was on it. And I literally do mean you will NEVER forget.

For the time being I suggest that you go and feed. Then get accustom to your new body. I know it can be overwhelming to discover all the changes. Luckily for you I had the desire and foresight to leave these notes. When I became a vampire I had to learn everything on my own. Trust me on this, these notes will prevent you a lot of needless pain and suffering. I hope you will seek me out. We vampires do enjoy company, as well as our old ways.

One last thing that you should know providing you want to survive. If you are getting hungry and cannot *access blood for whatever reason, solace can be found. You can temporarily lessen the desire for it with some wine. For some reason I have not been able to hash out, it seems to sustain us for a short period of time. Though it is not a replacement for the blood we need to survive. It is beneficial for short periods of time, between feedings. Also the longer that you live the longer before you need to feed.*

I think I've given you enough to think about for now. So I will at this point say goodbye. Come and visit with me, preferably sooner than later. I can save you a lot of grief, and missteps. Enjoy! ... Now go and eat, before you end up eating one of your friends.

Vladimir

Chase couldn't believe his eyes. He read the pages three times before setting them back into the hidden drawer and closing it. Well if what he had just read was true (and he was beginning to think it was), then he had a lot more explaining to do than he originally thought he did. But first he needed to eat. His stomach let loose a long low rumble to punctuate the thought. Chase got up from the table, and decided to go out to find something (someone) to eat.

Chase exited his house by the back door. He drifted down through town keeping to the shadows, seeking out his prey. He came across a number of people who were out and about. Whereas he seen them, they couldn't see him hidden deep in the shadows. Chase couldn't help marveling at the pure simplicity of it all. Chase decided on a lone female. He watched and followed her through the night waiting for the perfect time to strike.

As he watched and waited he observed the skinny little blonde stager along the streets. He could tell that she had obviously drunk a great deal. Judging from the foul smell drifting off of her, to Chase on some of the stronger gusts of wind. She had been drinking both wine, and port. She was dressed in a long grimy looking dress, covered with a tight fitting petticoat. She also looked and smelled as if she hadn't seen a bath in a number of days.

Over a period of an hour Chase realized she was looking for a place to lie down and fall asleep. As he followed her she made her way across town. Chase watched as she stopped every so often, when approached by a lone male. To Chase's disgust and surprise she was often lead off into an ally, by the male. He watched her get bent over garbage cans. As she was backed against walls, or laid down on piles of loose trash, and a couple of times onto her hands and knees. As he watched from the shadows, he saw her take the males into all three of her available openings. When the deed was done, the male handed her some coins, and they parted ways. Chase was disgusted and excited both, each time he watched her getting used.

Finally she was alone for a short period of time, and wandered off into a large clump of woods on the outskirts of town. As he drew nearer to her he watched her make a crude bed of juniper bows. He finally stepped out from his hiding place in the shadows to her left.

She looked up in surprise, smiled and said, "Well now hun, I was just getting ready for bed. But I could make an exception for you. What is it that would you like?"

Tilting his head slightly to the right Chase looked at her and replied. "Well that depends on what is being offered".

To his amazement the woman pulled on a couple of tie's on the front of her dress, freeing them. With a little wiggle of her hips the dress was soon pooled on the ground by her feet. She was left standing completely naked bathed in the silvery slants of moonlight penetrating the overhead tree's to bath the ground in its soft glow.

Smiling up at him she said, "All of this is yours for the taking, if you have the coin".

Chase pretended to look over her slim but well-shaped body as she turned around in small tight circles before him. Chase noted her firm perky breasts, narrow hips, high firm rear end, and dirty milky white skins. Smelling her blood and watching it pulse through a vein in her neck.

Chase licked his lips and asked, "What will it cost me for the whole package?"

As she was tired and pretty drunk, she couldn't remember how many men she had in her already. Though judging from how sore her arse, mouth and crotch felt, she guessed a fair number.

As she wasn't really interested in another round tonight she said, "For you hun I'll give you a deal. How does five dollars sound?"

Even in her drunken state she knew this was a very large amount to ask for. She was fully expecting him to cry off. Then go on a search for a cheaper piece of ass.

Pretending to think the number over Chase finally replied after a few seconds, "five dollars sounds like a fair number to me".

As this was a great deal of money for her, and not really believing he had it she said, "You'll have to pay first, then we'll get to it".

All too often she had done it the other way around. Only to receive nothing more for her efforts than a load of someone's spunk deposited into her. Hell it wasn't like she could go to the cops. They would only toss her into jail. Selling sex for money was illegal. She already had firsthand experience of that, having been arrested a number of times for it in the past. Chase fished the five dollars out of a pocket and handed it over to her with a smile on his face. She tucked the money into a pocket of her dress with the rest of the money she'd collect on the way to the forest.

Turning back to Chase she smiled and said, "How do you want to take me first?"

Chase led her to a nearby tree. Turned her to face it and told her to wrap her arms around it to hold on. He unfastened his trousers and let them slide down his long legs. Looking down he realized his manhood was hard and ready. Smiling Chase asked her what hole she wanted it in.

She replied, "Just pick one honey and slid into it, I like it in all of them".

Chase slid into her waiting vagina with a hard deep thrust of his hips.

She moaned at the sudden assault and said, "Damn hun your dick is big and cold. You gotta learn to keep it out of the drafts."

That was all the encouragement he needed to hear.

As Chase pumped in and out of her, he grabbed a handful of hair. Pulling on her hair lightly to the left; making her tilt her head out of the way to feed. She didn't protest at all, only obediently moving her head to where he wanted it. The big vein in the side of her neck seemed to jump out at him. As he watched it with his fresh new sight, he could actually see the blood flowing along to her heart. A second later he felt his teeth shifting. Chase wondered at the oddly pleasant sensation. Then felt the sharp pressure of his fangs pressing against his lower lip. Opening his mouth wide Chase reared his neck back as he continued to thrust hard and deep into her from behind.

He lowered his head in a lightning quick flash. The image of a rattlesnake flashed into his mind. Chase buried his elongated teeth into the exposed vein on the side of the neck and marveled at the simplicity of how easily his sharp teeth slipped into it. Her initial response was to try to pull away from him, but his strong grip on her head and his deep, hard pelvic thrusts kept her pinned to the tree. Chase marveled at the taste of her hot coppery blood and of its cooling effect on his hot, dry throat. As it quickly flowed into his mouth and down his throat, he swallowed her life into him as fast as he could. He could also clearly taste the salty sweet griminess of her little neck. The sensations were so overwhelming that he lost focus of himself for a short time.

He came back to himself when he heard the sharp, distinct sound of a bone snapping. Only then did he realize that he was pumping into her using his full, new vampire strength. The snapping bone must have been one in her pubic area; or her neck, broken by the angle of how it was pulled. Chase drank her life blood into himself as he continued to pump himself into her. As her heart stopped beating in her chest, Chase came deep inside her. As he pulled himself free of her now limp body. He noticed his manhood was covered in fresh blood, as he freed his sharp teeth from her cooling neck.

At first a pang of panic raced through his body. But it quickly passed as he realized that it was likely the case because he was a vampire. He could only assume at this point that instead of expelling semen he expelled mostly blood, as his body no longer produced much semen if any at all. Or it was just as likely that he had done some serious internal damage to her while having sex with her. His mind flashed back to the sound of the snapping bone. He would have to ask Vladimir if he ever met him. With any luck he would have an answer. Chase walked back over to the girls cloths and used them to clean the blood from him face as best as he could. Then he wiped him now limp manhood until it was clean. Chase walked back over to the girl with her cloths in his hands. Looking down on her corpse he emptied the money from her pocket into his, without taking the time to count it first. He dropped her now useless cloths onto her body, while he thought of what to do with her body.

After thinking for a short period of time he decided that he would ravage her body to make it look like she'd been attacked by a wild animal, in the night. Using his sharp teeth and finger nails he ripped her to shreds. Before tossing her dismembered body parts around her make shift campsite. He then took the time to wipe her blood off his body with her cloths, before redressing in his cloths. Who would have thought there was so much blood still in her body? Then he tore her clothing to shreds to make it look like the animal ate threw them to get at her soft body.

Marveling at how easy the whole process turned out to be, Chase made his way back into town. Wondering around for a while, Chase decided on a number of things. First he would go home and write a letter to Gail, and leave it on her porch for her to find in the morning. Second he was going to study the map in the chest and set out to find his creator. And third, for the time being at least he was going to keep the bar, and house. Fourth he was going to find the wine maker and learn what he could from him. By the time Chase had decided these things he was back home, and sitting at his kitchen table.

Chase wandered through his late father's study until he found some paper, ink, and some quills to write with. Sitting down at the desk in the room he began to write the letter.

Dear Gail,

I am having a hard time with the knowledge that it has been three day's since I've last seen you. A lot has changed since I've last seen you, however my feelings for you are not among them. I have and will continue to love you. That has not changed since we were both kids. Other than strengthening when we ran into each other again when I returned to town. You remember the chest of wine, and the book that was with it. Well let me say that they both opened my eyes in a whole new way.

I have been transformed as never before. And have gained a great deal of knowledge since we last spoke. I now know that it has in fact been three days since we last were together. However it honestly feels to me like mere hours. Please forgive me for my absence from you. I never intended to be away from you for more than a few hours at a time for the rest of my life. I still wish this were the case.

Ever since I first sat down with that strange little book to read; and those six bottles of wine, a couple of which I drank. Time seems to have taken on a whole new meaning for me. I still want to be with you forever, that has remained the same as well. But for the time being I will have to be apart from you; for just how long that will be I do not know. I cannot explain it to you right now, as I don't understand everything myself as of yet. I must go away for a period of time, to gain the knowledge I need. I hope it will be for only a very short time. Although like I already said, time is different for me now.

Now that I know what I must do and where I must go to get the answers and guidance I need. I must leave at once. I'd love nothing more than to see you again in person before I leave. But alas, I cannot allow that to happen in fear something should happen to you if I do. However the sooner I go the sooner I can return to your side. Believe me I know this doesn't seem to make sense to you. I'm still having a hard time with it all myself. I do hope to make it up to you when I have returned. ...If you will accept me back in your life at that time. I hope you will, when that time comes.

    I am enclosing the deed for the bar with this letter, as I am giving it to you. I wish that you will quit your current job (whatever that is, and I apologize for never asking you what it is), so that you can reopen and run the bar. If this is not something you're interested in doing, I'll understand. If that is the case, do with it as you see fit. Even if that means you decide to sell it. The key to the bar is also enclosed with this letter and the deed.

    I will return to you as soon as I can, if you're willing to see me at that time. Let me know by hanging a slip of blue fabric in one of your upstairs windows. If when I return I can see it hanging from the street, I'll know you still want me in your life. If it isn't visible I'll know that you want me to leave you alone, and will honor your wish.

    I will also leave with you a key for my house. That way if you decide to sell the bar, you will be able to. You will have access to the inventory and value logs my father left for me. So that you'll be able to get a fair value for the items in the bar, if the time comes and there are any questions raised. I will leave them on the bed in the bedroom you chose the night you stayed over, that way you can find them easily. I'll collect the key to the house when I return unless you would like to keep it. On the other hand if you don't want to see me when

I return, drop the key for the house through the mail slot of my front door.

I must depart soon, so will end here. I will have you in my heart and mind every second I'm away from you, until I return. And hope you will carry me in yours. Until I see you again. I swear to you I will return to you as quickly as I can. I also swear that if you accept me back into your life at that time. I will never leave your side for the remainder of your life.

I Love you always and forever,
Chase

Chase carefully folded the letter and left it on the desk. He searched through the desk drawers until he found some heavy paper to fashion an envelope from, and a stick of wax to seal it with. Some further searching produced the deed for the bar. It was tucked into another drawer of the desk along with the deeds to various other properties he inherited from his father. Chase decided to figure out what they were for at a later time. He needed to drop the letter of at Gail's while she was still asleep. He didn't want her to catch him. He didn't feel ready to reveal his secret to her as of yet. And in all honesty he did not trust himself enough to be around her yet, and not harm her.

Chase placed the letter, deed and keys on the center of the piece of paper and fashioned an envelope out if it around them. Heating the stick of wax with a candle until it began melting freely. He dropped a few large drops onto the paper where it joined to seal the envelope closed. He finished the process off by pressing his gold ring into the quickly cooling wax. Sitting back he marveled at how the blood red wax looked with his personal seal set into it.

Andy Elliott

Œ

When he had the ring crafted for his twenty-fifth birthday, it had never occurred to him to use it as a signet to seal letters. He just enjoyed the look of the first and last letters of his name, as they overlapped one another. Now seeing it used this way for the first time, he couldn't help but wonder why he'd never used it as such before.

Chase picked up the letter and returned to the kitchen to seek out the map at the bottom of the chest. He set the letter on the counter out of the way. He emptied the chest of all of its contents, and all of its packaging materials. True to the letter, there was indeed a map inscribed into the bottom of the chest. Bending low over the empty chest Chase studied it closely for well over an hour.

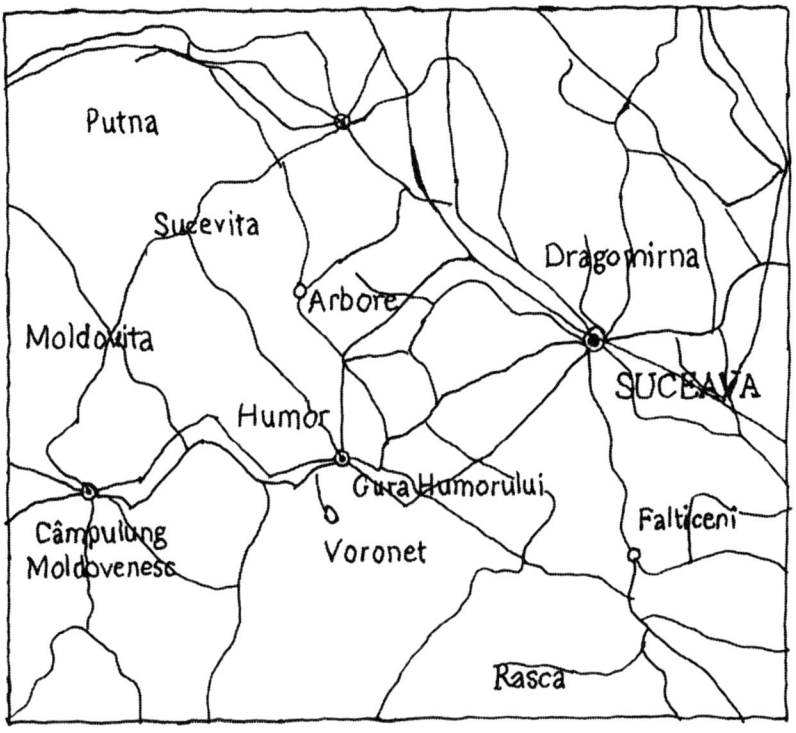

Before long Chase was walking outside to have one last cigarette.

Leaning against the railing of the back porch, Chase closed his eyes. He thought about the map, and the details he'd studied on it. Within seconds a complete picture of the map was forming behind his closed eyes. He was able to trace each and every road from start to end, as it was depicted on the map, at least he thought he could. Quickly finishing his smoke Chase disposed of the butt, and returned to the kitchen. He walked over to the chest and peered back inside it.

The map appeared before him as it had in his mind's eye. He felt confident that he would know where to go once he was in Romania. The only question left was which of the twelve locations listed on the map, was the one that he needed to go to in order to find the answers he needed. Looking closer at the entire inside of the chest Chase discovered a small depiction of a dragon in the left panel. Looking back at the map, he felt he knew where he had to go…Dragomirna.

Gathering up the account books from the den, and the ledger books from the basement Chase deposited them onto the bed as he told Gail he would in his letter. After which Chase quickly gathered a small ruck sack of cloths for the journey. To it he added all the available cash he had on hand left to him by his father, his wife, and the prostitute. Pulling the draw strings of the bag closed he left the house through the back door. Only stopping long enough to lock the door behind himself. His next scheduled stop was Gail's house. It had been a long time since he'd laid eyes on the big old homestead. But he recognized it at once, only the color of it had changed.

As he walked down Gail's street he was able to clearly see the old home, surrounded by shadows from the end of the road. Both floors were tightly wrapped in darkness. He could easily tell with his newly heightened senses that Gail was deeply asleep upstairs in her old bedroom. Softly snoring as she lay under her thick feather filled blanket. Even from a distance of half a block he could hear her steady heartbeat, and smell the sweet scent of her smooth skin. With each step closer to Gail's house his hunger rose. Seeing her before he left definitely was not an option. Stopping at the edge of the road in front of her house, his hunger for fresh blood was almost unbearable.

He already knew that his letter was going to break her heart even further. However he had no other options at the present time. He had to leave her at least until he was sure he wouldn't ravage her, and end her life in a fit of blood lust fueled rage. He silently walked onto her porch, and lovingly placed the envelope between her screen and front doors. He closed the screen door as silently as he'd opened it. He could hear Gail so clearly it was almost as if she was beside him. She continued to sleep deeply.

He turned and walked back down the block towards the outskirts of town. Chase felt it when she woke and rose from bed. Stopping at the end of the street, Chase turned to look back at Gail's house. As he watched a light went on in her bedroom. Then a second one lit up the downstairs front window. Within a few seconds he watched as her front door opened up. As he turned to walk away he watched as she bent down and picked up the envelope he left for her. It was out of his hands now, it was time to leave the future to fate. It was time to start the next leg of his new journey, and life.

Origins

Chase slowly walked out of town towards an unknown future, with the moon painting his back in a ghostly light. Within minutes he had disappeared into the shadows along the open road. He had no current means to get to Romania though it was obvious that he wasn't going to walk all the way there. Not only was the distance daunting, there was also a matter of the open waters he was forced to cross to get there. Being new with the whole vampire lifestyle, he had no idea if crossing water would be problematic. Though he knew he'd have to find out one way or the other.

As he was familiar with the surrounding area, he figured it would be as good a time to find out as any. Chase chose the location to veer off the road into the woods along the left hand side. Chase knew traveling a few hundred feet into the woods would bring him to a fairly shallow pond. Chase had spent many hours as a child fishing and swimming in the pond. Now he figured it would serve as his testing ground. It was as good a time to figure out if he could swim or sink, literally, as any.

Chase soon walked into a little clearing at the edge of the pond. To his pleasant surprise there was a fallen tree within easy reach of the water's edge. Chase quickly dropped his bag, stripped off his clothing and walked out into the water. The temperature of the water was meaningless to him. He didn't feel it like he did not long ago. It was pleasantly warm as he waded out into the deeper water. When his hips were covered with the warm water of the pond, he stopped to look around. Only his progression out into the silvery liquid marred the still surface of the pond.

Judging where he was as good a spot for his experiment as any, he took a deep breath and dove under the surface of the water. Moving his arms and legs in his familiar swimming pattern, he moved out into the still water. Marveling at the way the water moved across his naked flesh he kept swimming. A few strokes further he figured he'd better return to the surface for some air. Breaking free of the surface, Chase stopped his forward movement and treaded water. He couldn't believe his eyes at first. He was over half way across the small pond.

Well that answered that question. Vampires could swim, and swim well apparently. He had never in life been able to swim that far that fast. Nor without needing to return to the surface to breath in more air, or any air at all. Come to think of it, he was still holding his breath. Over ten long minutes had to have passed since he dove under water. Then again the more he thought of it, he didn't remember breathing since waking up. So vampires didn't need to breathe air either, good to know. Taking a deep breath of air in through his nose; for no other reason than because he could. Chase could smell the rotten earth and foliage scents of the forest. And the stale stagnate odor of the pond he was swimming in.

This was a newly found ability he was going to enjoy. Never again would he be forced to endure the putrid stench of foul odors around him. He vowed to himself then and there to only breathe when trying to fit in with humans. Or if he really needed to breathe for a specific reason, such as in order to track food. Just like that the memory clicked into place. He had breathed since awakening. He remembered smelling the girl he had feed off in the woods. Chase swam back to shore and walked out of the pond slowly. He quickly jogged around the small clearing until his body was completely dry. Fortunately with his new vampire abilities it only took a matter of seconds. After which he quickly redressed and headed back to the open road.

Chase was walking down the side of the road for hours. Watching the area around him for signs of life, with very little to note other than the odd small animal. Hours later the road became little more than a broken trail, winding through some dense dark woods. With no other options Chase continued along it heading into the east. Sooner or later he would reach the coast line of the Atlantic Ocean. Though he had no way of knowing how far from it he actually was. However he figured it would take him weeks to reach it, walking the entire way.

He would have to see about finding a worthy horse to ride. Or some other form of transportation. Even though walking no longer tired him out, it was still hard on his boots. While walking he listened to the night as he passed through it. Seeking to understand his new abilities, and learn what he could about them on his own. The trees began to overtake the road the further along the path he walked. Soon they were brushing up against him and the path disappeared altogether.

A branch ran along his arm opening up a deep scratch. Chase stopped and looked at his arm in awe. One second there as a deep gash running the length of his right forearm. Dark amber blood oozed from the opening in his flesh. The sight of the flowing blood made his stomach lurch, and his mouth water. The next second it was completely healed up, without so much as a trace of a scar. So he was able to heal almost instantly. Wicked… he brushed the dried blood from his arm absently. He began to wonder how impervious he was to physical damage. He'd have to ask his mysterious blood donor when they met. As he figured this was one question that could easily be deadly to acquire the answer to on his own.

He'd resumed walking as he thought. It soon became apparent to him that he was thinking too deeply when he heard noise around him in the woods on three sides. Seconds before three men stepped out of the trees around him. If he was still a mere human he would have been in trouble. It was easy to tell from their appearances that they meant to do him harm. All three men wore dirty long black coats covering even dirties black jeans and shirts. And all three of them had a pistol in their hands pointed at his chest.

"Well now, fellows, look what we have here," the guy directly in front of Case said. "I think we'll have some fun tonight after all. And here I was beginning to think it was going to be a boring night."

"Yeah, it was getting boring wandering around these woods" the guy laughing to his left added.

"So now, fella, how's about you hand over all your money," the guy on the right chimed in. "And while you're at it, unbuckle that gun belt and let it fall to the ground."

Knowing he had nothing to fear from these fools, Chase decided to play along for a bit. He unbuckled his gun belt and let it fall to his feet.

The guy in front of him told him to take three big steps back and stop. Chase took three long, slow strides backwards away from the men, and his gun.

The guy on the right stepped forward, holstered his gun, and picked up Chase's gun belt, smiling at Chase as he strapped it on "Thanks for the new gun. Mine was getting kinda worn out."

It was clear that he wanted Chase to respond.

"You have my gun, and you can have my money," Chase told him. "Though I should really warn the three of you, you really should rethink what you're doing before you all get hurt or worse."

The guy in the middle laughed so hard that tears ran down his cheeks. "Look out, boys! We got a tough guy here. He's gonna take his gun back, and go on his merry little way."

Chase just smiled at them. "I'll take more than my gun from you fools before we part ways. When I walk away I'll be the only one left standing on my feet, and alive."

While the three men looked at him like he was insane, Chase widened his smile a little and said, "I am going to break your nose and neck". To the man to his right and left, "And I am going to drain your body of every ounce of blood", to the man right in front of him.

That was enough to make the three of them charge at him. Chase felt his teeth lengthen within his mouth. Within mere seconds Chase had dealt with the first two men as he had told them he would, and was drinking the blood from the third. When the body was finally drained of all its blood, Chase let it drop to the ground. Walking over to one of the other lifeless bodies, Chase picked it up and sank his fangs into its cooling neck. The blood didn't taste right to him, it was almost like it had turned bad within the few minutes it had stopped flowing through the man's veins. He soon dropped the lifeless body back onto the ground and spit the blood out of his mouth. He tried to drink the blood from the other man, but had the same result. The blood just didn't taste right to him from a corpse.

Well that settled that. In order to be desirable the blood had to come from a live source. Otherwise it tasted flat and slightly rancid to him. He wondered if he could drain some blood from a live host into a container for later drinking. He would have to try it some time to find out for sure. It was not going to be a possibility at present. Not with all three of the men currently already being dead. Too bad, a bit more fresh blood might not have been a bad thing. So what to do with the bodies this time?

The ground was soft enough to dig a hole to put them in. But that would be a lot of work without a shovel. Two of them were still full of blood, so ripping them apart would be really messy. Oh, what to do? Listening to the sounds of the woods, Chase heard a pack of wolves off to the right about a mile or so away. He could carry the bodies closer to them and open them up so they could smell the blood. If they were hungry enough they would eat them. And from the sounds of them, they were. Not that he could ever pretend to know anything about wolves.

Chase took his gun belt back from the dead body and strapped it back around his waist. He then checked their pockets for other useful items. He came across a few crumpled up bills and a handful of change. He added the meager three dollars and twenty seven cents to his own pocket, as there was no reason to leave it for someone else to claim if or when someone came across their remains. Also a large knife was strapped to the hip of one of the bodies. He claimed this for himself, figuring it might come in handy at some point. There was little else of value, even the guns looked cheap and near the end of the usage, their bullets were the wrong caliber for his gun. As such they were useless to him also. He left them strapped to the bodies.

Chase was surprised that he could easily pick up and carry all three bodies at once. He carried them to within a hundred feet of the wolf pack and placed them quietly on the ground. Not wanting to scare the wolves away. Using his new knife he sliced open the three bodies to free the scent of their innards, and blood. He could hear the wolves sniffing in the direction of the bodies and quickly left the area so as not to frighten them off. He stopped when he reached the spot where he encountered the men. Looking around the area, he was satisfied with the sounds of the hungry wolves tearing into the freshly dead bodies he had served up for them. Satisfied that the area was indeed clear of almost all signs anyone had been there, other than some blood which would soon fade from sight.

Chase began to walk east once more when he heard the wolves fighting over the fresh meat, and eating it with more enthusiasm, while thinking to himself that he was really going to enjoy being a vampire. Shortly thereafter he exited the woods. A few steps later he found another trial leading off to the east and decided to follow it. He still had no idea where he was, though judging from the position of the sun in the sky. He had to of travelled a large distance throughout the night. He figured it might not take him as long to reach the ocean as he originally thought it would.

Chase wandered further and further east throughout the day. Other than the odd look from a local he went unchallenged. By night fall of that day he began to smell the salty scent of the ocean. Luckily he was traveling along the road with a strange woman at the time. If he hadn't of been trying to pretend to be human he would have never smelt the ocean's scent. The woman he was traveling with was like no other he had ever met. Even with his new abilities she didn't smell like other women did. Though he couldn't place why, although he was sure there had to be a valid reason. Although it was not the sort of thing he could come right out and ask her.

For some strange reason this strange woman made something inside him stir. He couldn't put his finger on it, but he felt it as soon as he met her. It was around noon hour. He had just left the last little village about half an hour before coming across her. As he was walking along the road he decided to lean against a tree along the side of the road, for a short break. As he had been walking for what seemed like hours already. Whereas he wasn't the least bit tired, he desired a change of pace. He was watching a small deer across the road in a field, eating some grass. He was just making up his mind to track and kill the deer, just for the change of pace, and to find out what deer blood tasted like. Not that he was the least bit hungry. He had only arrived at this conclusion because he had been watching the deer and the though entered his mind.

Now that he had the idea he couldn't help but wonder if he could sustain himself off of animal blood if he found human blood to be in short supply. As it might ultimately mean his prolonged survival, he figured it was well worth his taking the time to find out.

The next thing he realized a strange woman walked up beside him and stopped. She had flowing light red hair that fell to her waist. It was tied back with a couple of brightly colored scarves. She was dressed in an ankle length deep purple gown, covered with an open blood red cloak of the same length as her gown. When she stopped Chase noticed that she was about a head and a half shorter than he was. She was slender in a pleasant way, with medium sized firm, upward tilting breasts. The cut of her gown left the top portion of her breast out for display. Chase knew if he had still been a mortal man, he would have been sexually attracted to her.

Their eyes meet once his had finished their slow inquisitive search over her shapely body, before they finally come to rest on her pretty young face.

This strange young woman said, "I think we should walk together for a while. I'm going to the next village, and could use some company. Are you willing to walk with me?"

Chase was awe struck. Never in his life had any female ever presented herself to him like this. And now that he was a vampire it seemed to him to be an even stranger request.

He knew that since becoming a vampire his looks had changed enough that no mere human would freely approach his as she had. All other people he had seen and left alive had given him a wide berth. Many of which had quickly turned their heads as soon as their eyes took him in. It was almost as if they could easily see he was a predator to be avoided at all costs.

Shaking his head in disbelief he replied, "These are dangerous roads to be traveling, while dressed like that. Even more so when you walk up to a stranger and ask them to walk with you. You are either very brave or something else. I'll walk with you for a spell if you wish. However I'm not much of a talker, and I won't wait for you if you can't keep up with me".

To which she responded, "A spell it shall be then. Though I am not very brave, I can tell you're a good person to travel with. As such I know I will make it to my home without issue. I'll keep up with you easily, as I don't tire very easily. Also I don't talk much, and prefer to think as I walk. As we will be spending the next few days together, you can call me…Dawn…like the early morning light".

Chase felt the strange sensation beginning to course through his body at this point. For some unexplainable reason he felt like Dawn and he were connected somehow.

Smiling back at her Chase said, "Sounds good to me. Let's get going then, so we can get you home in good time".

Headed back out onto the road, they walked along in almost complete silence. Chase has completely forgotten the deer by this point. They only exchanged words a few times for the majority of their walking.

As the darkness deepened Chase decided he would spare the poor girl the aggravations of walking, almost blind, through the inky black darkness of the night. Though she had never mentioned stopping, and did not appear to be bothered by the idea of continuing, nor did she seem tired.

Looking over at Dawn; Chase said, "How's about we find a place to camp for the night. It's getting too dark to see much, and your looking like you could use some sleep".

Dawn smiled over at Chase and replied, "That sounds like a wonderful idea. How's about if we look for a place a little further up the road? I think I can manage to trudge along for at least an hour longer. But if we find a good spot before then we'll stop then".

With that decision made, they continued further down the road.

They only went about twenty minutes further down the road, before a large open field appeared up the road a little further off on the right hand side.

Chase looked over at Dawn and said, "Well that looks like a great place to stop for the evening. We will be able to see anyone coming for miles, if we set up camp for the night in the middle of the field".

Dawn agreed with the idea and they turned off the road into the field a short time later. Before an hour was up, the camp had been set-up and they were relaxing beside a small camp fire.

They shared out some food that Dawn had in the folds of her dress and talked into the night. They made plans for the upcoming day. Chase had no idea as to where they even where. However Dawn figured they were within a day's walk of Quebec. Dawn informed Chase that she would be parting with him there as it was where she lived. She'd also told him he would be more than welcome to join her there for a little while to rest and regain his strength if he wished to. Chase did not want to give himself away as being anything less than human. Told her he would let her know how he felt when the time came.

Chase told her to go to sleep, and that he would take the first watch, to make sure no one snuck up on them as they slept. Dawn said she was too tired to argue about it. She rolled up in her trail blanket, turned away from the fire and quickly fell asleep. Chase moved further away from her, there was something about her that set his nerves on edge. He couldn't identify it, but that didn't make the feeling any less real. As he pondered what it was about her he wandered around the area, not paying any attention to where he was, or going to end up.

Thinking it over Chase reflected that she smelled of roses, lavender, cinnamon, and cloves. Though there was nothing in her smell that bothered him. It was something else. She was pleasant and friendly. They talked from time to time to help fill the quiet and loneliness of the open road, but not remotely enough to turn him against her for it. There was also the mystery of where she was concealing all the items she came up with when require. The food they had eaten, the bed roll, the matches to start the fire. Though she did not carry a sack, pack or bag of any kind that his keen eyes could see. And she appeared far too slender to easily conceal it undetected by his vampiric sight upon her person. She never the less came up with the items somehow.

The sound of the blood running through her veins was a welcome distraction to him. However not so much that she was at risk of him attacking and draining her. The fact that her blood did not call to the endless hunger within him, only served to further confuse him. However rather than making him feel uneasy about it, it made him feel more comfortable and relaxed around her. It gave him hope that he could become that way around Gail as well.

He just couldn't place it. Pushing the thought aside he decided to concentrate on getting her to Quebec so he could leave her side. Before being with her could cause him any further distractions that would prolong his separation from Gail. She continued to plague his mind no matter what else was bouncing around within it. During his thinking and wandering, he realized after pushing his thoughts away that he had wandered a fair distance from their little camp. He could see Dawn's apparently slumbering form silhouetted by the small camp fire. Though he was too far from her for her to see him if she were to awaken. Chase started walking back to the camp, so she wouldn't have to worry about if he left her if she were to awaken.

He'd only made it about half way back when something moved in the shadows off to his right. Chase stopped dead in his tracks and peered into the night at a little bush. As it was the only likely place for the movement to have come from without his being able to clearly see what it was that moved. As he stood there watching a figured came into view from behind the bush. At the same time a cloud moved in front of the moon, rendering Chase's ability to see who it was more clearly impossible. The overcast night was so dark when the moon was hidden behind a cloud that even with his vampiric sight Chase was almost blind. Had he of been still completely human he wouldn't be able to see more than a foot in front of himself.

The figure made slow deliberately menacing strides towards Chase. When the shadowy figure was almost ten feet away the cloud moved from in front of the moon. At the same instant Chase could see the tall figure of a man clearly. Though the night was dark, with his heightened sight, Chase could make out every feature of the man. He stood approximately the same height as Chase did. He was dressed in a long dirty trail coat and dusty cowboy hat. Nothing about the man's appearance caused Chase a moment of concern. Not even the big revolver sitting firmly in the man's right hand.

The man stopped five feet short of Chase and said, "you shouldn't have wandered so far from your little lady friend over there. But seeing as you did, it'll make things easier for me".

Blinking at the man Chase replied, "Look mister I don't want any problems. Why don't you turn around and go back from where you came before it is too late".

Laughing the man said to Chase, "you don't want any trouble you say. I need to walk away. Are you dumb or something buster? I'm the one with the gun drawn, and pointed. What you need to do is lie down on the ground and put your face in the dirt".

When Chase didn't move the man took a step closer to him and said, "I said lay down on the ground. You had better do it before I change my mind and just shoot you".

Laughing softly in return Chase said, "Oh, you can shoot me. Hell you can empty all the bullets in your gun into me. But it isn't going to change the fact that you will be just as dead if you don't walk away now".

The stranger couldn't believe what he was hearing.

Shaking his head he said to Chase, "Fine have it your way. You could have lived the night out, but now you'll die. I don't know why some people gotta be so stupid".

Moving his thumb only, the man reached to cock the hammer of the gun as he stared deep into Chase's eyes. Before the hammer was fully cocked, Chase had closed the distance between the two of them. Chase grabbed the man's coat in one hand, and the gun in the other. Chase drove his fangs into the man's neck at the same time he crushed his hand. The twisted gun hit the ground mere seconds before the man's dead body did.

Cursing to himself softly, Chase picked up the gun, looked at it in shock and disbelief. He had never realized he was now strong enough to mangle a gun so completely, so easily. Chase threw it as far as he could away from the little camp. More surprising to himself as he watched the crumpled wreck sail through the air, until it could no longer be seen; that he could throw something so far. A few seconds later he heard the soft thump in the far distance as it landed on the ground. Looking back towards the camp, to see if the brief encounter had awakened Dawn; Chase was thankful for his new vampiric vision. He quickly noted that she still appeared to be sleeping, before bending down to pick up the lifeless body. Chase turned from the camp and carried the corpse further into the wastelands.

He stopped at some dense shrubs and dumped the body onto a low bush. Chase dug a shallow grave within a few seconds. His strong fingers easily plunging into the hard packed ground, and deposited the corpse into it. Chase checked all of the pockets for anything of value. Other than seventeen dollars the man had nothing else of value. Chase covered the body over and turned back towards camp. Within a couple of minutes he was once again sitting beside the little fire. As if nothing at all had just taken place.

Chase was just placing a few more small branches into the dwindling flames when Dawn began to stir. Dawn sat up a few minutes later, and smiled at Chase as she stretched.

Chase said, "I hope you had a good sleep. Though you could have slept a while longer, I would have woken you when I got tired".

Dawn gave him a sharp look of reproach and said, "I've had plenty of rest already. If I'd have rested any longer the morning would be on us before you got any sleep. I'm fine now so you can get some sleep, I'll take watch".

Chase finished feeding the remaining sticks into the flames, building the fire up so Dawn could see better, then laid down on his back and closed his eyes. He was not going to go to sleep, but it was not above him to pretend to. He laid under his camp blanket for the remainder of the night listening to Dawn moving about. As he pretended to sleep Chase watched Dawn through narrowly silted eyes as she collected more little branches and sticks from the nearby area. All the while muttering to herself so quietly under her breath that even with his heightened hearing he couldn't understand a word she was saying. He figured she was singing to herself as the rhythm of her muttering had a sort of sing-song quality to it. As the sun was just clearing the trees off to the east Dawn tapped his foot to wake him up with the end of a stick. A short while later they had repacked their meager camp. They had started walking again with only a few words being said between them.

As she had forecasted, they reached Quebec later that afternoon. It appeared to be a run down dirty little village to Chase. He couldn't see himself being happy to live within its borders. The few people they passed along the way to Dawn's house gave them dirty looks before hurrying along their way. Chase could hear a number of different people talking however couldn't understand a word anyone was saying as they were speaking in some weird language. Within a few minutes Dawn stopped in front of a large two story house and claimed that it was hers. She invited him inside, as she turned and walked towards the front door. Chase figured it would be in his interest to stop and visit with her for a little while. To his way of thinking it would further help him pretend to be human. Also for some reason he didn't feel like it was time yet for him to leave her side. But that he guessed was due to the strange connection he felt towards her. After all they had travelled a long distance together before arriving at her door. Turning towards the house he followed her to the door, then through it.

As she stepped inside Dawn turned on a light, before stepping to the side to allow Chase to walk past her further into the house.

Dawn closed the door, and said, "Go straight down the hall and you'll walk into the kitchen. I'll make you something hot to eat, and get you a nice cold drink".

She passed Chase just inside the kitchen door, turned on a light and told him to have a seat at the table. A few minutes later she sat a large glass of chilled red wine on the table in front of Chase and a second one in front of an empty chair opposite of him.

Dawn placed a bowl of mixed fruit and berries on the table and a small bowl full of assorted nuts beside it. Before returning to the other side of the room to fetch a plate full of thinly sliced raw venison.

As she placed it in the middle of the table she sat down and said, "I don't know if you've ever had venison this way but it is a favorite of mine. It's raw, thinly sliced with just a faint sprinkling of salt and pepper on it for flavor".

Chase smiled and replied, "No, I've never tried it that way before but I'm sure it will be wonderful".

Chase used a fork that he didn't remember seeing her place in front of him. Chase took one of the thinly sliced pieces of meat from the plate. Sniffing it first made his mouth water. It smelled strangely of the wild and of blood. He eagerly took a small bite from it, not wanting to look foolish if his body rejected it being in his mouth. To his pleasant surprise it tasted wonderful, and soon had him wanting more of it.

They ate in relative silence, and drank a couple of glasses of wine each before Dawn said, "It is getting late, and I know I'm dead tired. Why don't you stay in my spare bedroom tonight? I'm sure your bones would enjoy a break from sleeping on the hard ground".

After a few seconds consideration Chase accepted the offer. Dawn showed him to a spare room and bade him a goodnights sleep. Chase closed the door behind him, and walked deeper into the room. It had the same strange smell as Dawn did. Though it didn't make him feel the same way she did, it was clear that this room served as more than just a spare bedroom for her. Though from the look of it he had no clear idea of what that could be.

Though the only things in the room were a small flat topped dresser and a large four-poster bed, it had a welcome homey feeling to it. Chase kicked off his boots, stripped off his clothing and lay down on the bed naked. As he wasn't going to sleep he merely laid down on top of the blankets rather than under them. Come morning when he heard Dawn moving around the house he would mess the bed up to make it look like he had slept in it. Then again on second thought as a guest in the house it would only be respectful of him to make the bed in the morning, he reasoned. Therefore it would render the need to mess the bed up redundant.

The night passed by slowly, Chase lay on top of the bed listening to the sounds of Dawn sleeping in her bed down the hallway. Shortly after five in the morning Chase heard Dawn get out of bed. He listened to her moving around her bedroom for about fifteen minutes before she left it for what he figured would be the day. She lingered outside of his closed door for a few minutes, no doubt listening to hear if he was asleep or not. She then went downstairs and into the kitchen. A short time later Chase could smell freshly made coffee, and decided it was time to pretend to get up himself.

After moving around the room for a few minutes, he pretended to make the bed. Chase dressed and wandered downstairs and into the kitchen. He accepted a cup of coffee, and sat drinking it while he and Dawn talked. Dawn told him about the history of the town, and that of her family. During which she explained that the people of the town spoke a language called

French. No wonder it had sounded so strange to him he thought. It had been the very first time he had ever heard it spoken, or heard of the language. Though Chase could tell there were things she was keeping from him. He told her a little about himself and of his history in return. Making sure he left out the part about becoming and being a vampire of course. That was information he felt best that she didn't need know. He couldn't judge her well enough to know what her reaction would be. And he didn't want to half to kill her if she took it badly. He had come to like her, also there was the fact that a fair number of people seen her let him into her house.

A couple of hours later Chase announced to Dawn that he felt like a new man after the good night's sleep he had gotten. He thanked her for her hospitality and for the usage of her room, and bed. He accepted a moderate sized package of what she termed "trail food", and said fair well to Dawn.

As he walked towards the edge of her property she called to him, "make sure to stop by and see me the next time you're in the area. You'll always be welcome within my walls".

Chase thanked her and assured her that he would, before turning towards the open road once more.

The rest of the journey to the ocean was uneventful. He ate when he needed to, or when he was pestered by some would be thief. He rested when he felt like taking a break from walking, although he wasn't tired. By the time the ocean came into view in the distance a little over a month had passed. Even though to Chase it felt more like a matter of hours.

Three days later Chase was standing on a wharf talking to a man working out the details for passage on a steamship to Romania. The man informed Chase that a lot of strange things were happening in that strange land. As such there weren't many ships willing to drop anchor in the Romanian ports. He claimed that he knew of only one ship in the area that would go there and drop anchor. The sailor continuously tried to talk Chase out of making the trip there. Repeatedly stating how unsafe a place it was to be. Chase fed him a tale that he had an uncle who had been living there for majority of his life. And how he had received word that the uncle had unexpectedly died, and left him a large inheritance. Chase attempted to reassure the sailor that if not for needing to go there in person to collect the inheritance he would definitely heed his warnings and not make the trip.

Chase tried to implore upon him that he had no other choice but to go there. Hastily adding that he had no real desire for the inheritance and would forgot the whole thing if not for his own mother, who was forcing him to go. As she claimed that the uncle was her only brother and had a lot of money and power in Romania. And that she would never speak to him again if he was to be so foolish as to pass over the generous gift her brother was giving him. Chase confided to the sailor that he seriously doubted that the inheritance would be worth what the cost of the trip was costing him. However he told him his mother's health was failing her and she would likely pass on herself in the next year or two, so he had to keep her happy. Otherwise she was planning on writing him out of her own will, in which as she had told him; she currently was leaving him her own considerable estate. Chase sheepishly admitted that he was not willing to lose that.

After almost an hour and three hundred dollars later, Chase had the name of the ship, and its captain. Chase suspected that he could have gotten the same information for free had he of given the sailor some tale of great lose and poverty. However the fee did not bother him as he could get all the money he needed or could ever want whenever need be. Shortly thereafter Chase located the ship further down the wharf. The captain was standing alongside his ship smoking a pipe when Chase walked up to him. After a short conversation Chase handed the captain the five hundred dollars he demanded to make the voyage. As soon as he had the money in hand the captain called a deck hand and directed him to show Chase to his private cabin.

The ship pulled out of port almost an hour later, once the last passenger had boarded. At supper later that night Chase came to learn he was one of twenty-five passengers aboard the little ship.

Andy Elliott

Destiney

The ocean crossing aboard Destiney was slow paced with many stops. Chase quickly learned that had he paid a good deal more money to the captain he could have had a private voyage across the ocean. However the frequent stops and constantly changing passengers aboard the ship worked in Chase's favor. When they pulled into a port and spent the night he was able to slip ashore and hunt.

He was also able to meet and learn a great deal about majority of the passengers while they were aboard the ship. A large number of them were fairly wealthy, lived alone, and had no family. Chase made a point of getting as close to these passengers as he could. Chase strived to become as friendly with them as he could. Once he had done that he secured himself an invitation to their house when they pulled into their respective ports.

When they made the stops at all the various ports Chase would make a point to be handily near the gangway when his potential target was getting ready to leave the ship to go home. Chase would strike up a conversation with them as soon as he could and walk off the ship beside them. They almost always tried to make a point of trying to sell Chase on the finer points of their respective little city, town, or village. They also always made a point of once more extending their offer for him to accompany them to their homes. Chase always made a point of accepting their offer after which he would accompany them to their homes.

Once there if he liked the house he would get to know more about the person, before he drained them quickly of their blood. He removed anything of value from their corpses then dispatched of the body far from the house. After which he would return to the house to quickly search through it, to learn if the contents within them of any real value to him. If there were any pictures of the now deceased, previous owner he would destroy them.

When this task was finally done he would record the person's name, the location of the house and the address into a little booklet he took to carrying with him. That way he could keep track of his various identities and possessions for future use, if he chose to at some point in time. Once all that was completed he would find the deed for the house, and any other properties, money and keys for the houses. After locking the houses up, he would return to the ship with his newly obtained possessions.

After a while he had amassed a large number of deeds, keys, and money. He figured it was time for him to get something to safely keep them all in so as he wouldn't have to carry them all or leave them unsecured but well hidden within his cabin on the ship. As luck would have it they pulled into a busy harbor one sunny afternoon. The captain informed the passengers that the ship would remain in the port until sundown in three days' time, to allow time to restock the ship. And get a few minor repairs before departing once more.

The captain told everyone on board that if they were not back onboard the ship when the time came to head back out onto the open waters, he would not wait for them. Nor would he be held responsible for them or any of their belongings remaining on the ship. If they did not return to the ship before he set sail once more. Once his short but fierce speech was finished the captain gave orders to run out the gangway. So those wanting to return to land could, before he returned to his cabin.

Chase was one of the first passengers off the ship. He quickly located a shop that sold steamer trunks. After searching through the entire inventory he settled on a heavy black cherry chest. He was drawn to it partly due to the color of the wood, the weight of the chest, the detailed carvings covering all the outer panels, and the thick silver lining inside of the chest. Chase also like the deep large lift out section, also fashioned from a thick heavy sheet of silver. The chest was almost identical to the chest he had at home. But it was accented with silver instead of gold. The shop owner stated that they had hand made the piece a number of years before. The piece had been a special order for a customer who never returned for it. Unfortunately due to the high price of the item, not too many people could afford to purchase it.

Chase stated that he would be more than happy to purchase it. The only condition being that the shop owner fashion either a clasp mechanism that a lock could be fastened to; or by installing a locking mechanism onto it prior to sunset the next night. Chase explained to the shop owner that he was due to leave from port at that time, and had need of it for the journey. He figured he would give himself two days' grace to ensure he had the chest in time. Also to allow himself time to feed and do some other shopping without having to rush around. The shop owner was tripping over himself with joy, at the thought of the small fortune the sale would give him. He assured Chase that he would have the chest ready for him in the mere one days' time frame Chase had imposed upon him. The shop keeper informed Chase that he would complete the required work himself to ensure nothing held up the order.

Chase thanked the man and promised to return the next day for his chest. Only at this point in time did Chase think to ask how much the finished chest would cost him. After a few minutes thought the shop keeper told Chase it would cost a hefty six hundred dollars. Chase knew the cost had been highly inflated because he was a stranger, and because of the added work the shop keeper had to do to it before he could sell it. But he figured the cost was that high mainly because he had only asked for the price almost as an afterthought. Chase did a quick mental calculation on how much money he had either on him or stashed back onboard the ship. He figured the six hundred dollars would put a small dent into his ready supply of cash, but he could hardly get by without a chest much longer. The shop keeper was looking more and more nervous the longer Chase took to respond.

Just as he was about to say something further, Chase smiled broadly and said, "I have thought long and hard. I have no other choice but to agree that is a very fair price. However I will pay you three hundred dollars right here and now. To ensure you I will return for the chest. And I will pay the remainder when I return tomorrow to pick up the finished chest. I will warn you though if my chest is not completed when I return. Or if it is not done to the same high level of quality the rest of the chest is. I will collect my three hundred dollars back from you with interest".

As Chase reached into one of his various pockets and pulled out a thick wad of bills the shop keeper promised over and over again that the chest would be ready as promised with only the finest quality of workmanship going into it.

He was so befuddled by Chase not turning him down flat or trying to haggle over the price as most other people would, he also stated in a fit of bragging, "If I do not make the additions as you have ordered to your desired quality level. You can take the chest and owe me not one cent more for it".

Only after the words had left his mouth did the shop keeper realize what he had just said. If it was not for the fact that he prided himself on being a man of his words. He would have taken back his last statement. As it were he seriously began to worry for the first time that the stranger truly liked the finished chest. Otherwise he had just talked himself out of three hundred dollars of pure profit.

Handing the shop keeper the stated three hundred dollars Chase smiled and said, "I will hold you to that, as you can hold me to my words. I will return for my chest tomorrow, and am sure I will not be disappointed".

Chase left the shop and quickly crossed the street to another shop. He needed some clothing, as his current ones were beginning to wear out and looked rather poor for a man of his station of life. Or at least of the station of life he was in the process of creating for himself.

Chase purchased a new trail coat of soft black leather, a new rawhide black cowboy hat. Five pairs of pants, a belt, a number of pairs of socks, underwear, and five long sleeved button-up shirts; each of a different color. After paying for his purchase Chase asked the woman in the shop to wrap them up, and hold them for him until he returned from picking up his chest. For a few more dollars the woman was happy to do so.

By the time Chase had finished trying on and being fitted for his new cloths. After buying his clothing two hours had passed. Chase visited a number of other shops in the little port. Buying trivial things here or there as the mood hit him. The last shop he visited was loaded with various guns and ammunitions. Chase really didn't need the gun he already wore on his hip. He had to admit to himself that he truly did enjoy the weight and look of the gun as it hung uselessly there. Chase decided on buying a matching gun and gun belt to hang from the other hip. After trying on the second gun belt and standing in front of a full length mirror he liked the way it looked on him.

Along with enough bullets to fill all the chambers of both guns, and every bullet slot built into both of the gun belts. Leaving the gun shop Chase returned to the ship for the night. As he lay in his narrow bed listening to the sounds onboard the ship, Chase decided that he would also buy himself a pair of new boots in the port to complete his new outfits. Chase spent the better part of the next day searching the port for a pair of boots that he liked. He finally came to the conclusion that he was not going to find any. The little port village simply did not sell cowboy boots at all. Although he quickly found out that he could buy almost any other imaginable kind. With an air of utter defeat he returned to the little shop for his chest at the prearranged time. The shop keeper was happy to see that he had returned. As promised the chest was ready for him. Chase could see the chest sitting on the floor with two banded straps added to it.

The shop keeper told Chase he had fashioned the bands and the locks out of solid gold. He told Chase he would have made them from silver as well but it would turn black if left in the open air for a period of time. And that the salted air close to open water was very hard on silver and made it tarnish faster. Even though he admitted that there was already a good deal of silver accenting the chest. Chase told him that the gold was an excellent addition, and commended him on the craftsmanship of the entire chest. To himself Chase noted that the shop keeper had also taken the time to etch a subtle simple design into the gold straps and onto the face of the lock.

Chase asked how much he owed for the chest. Even though he clearly recalled that he only owed an additional three hundred dollars for the completed chest. The shop keeper lowered his head and mumbled three hundred into his chest. If Chase was not a vampire he never would have heard him. A blind man could clearly tell the shop keeper was unsure if he was going to get the remaining amount or if he was in for an argument.

Smiling Chase said, "Was that three hundred dollars?"

The shop keeper turned deep red and nodded his head several time before looking up to Chase. Chase could clearly see the embarrassment in the man's eyes. He knew the shop keeper was a good man by the looks of him. And that he was feeling guilty about taking advantage of him by charging him such a steep price.

Smiling even more Chase laughed and said, "That sounds like a very fair price to me. And I feel the need to tell you that you did a wonderful job modifying the chest as I requested. Also that it is good to have the pleasure to deal with a fine craftsman that is good to his word. A lesser man would have tried to soak me for even more money than we agreed upon".

Chase reached into his pocket for the money. Smiling broadly himself the shop keeper watched as Chase counted out a number of bills, paused a second or two before counting out a few more bills, folded them and handed them to the shop keeper.

As his fingers closed over the large wad of paper Chase said, "I've added an extra hundred for your willingness to add the locking mechanism in such a short time. Also for doing such a fine job in doing so. To me the chest looks like it had originally been made that way and not modified at all".

The shop keeper tried to protest and give the extra money back.

Laughing Chase stated, "I'll have none of that. I've more than enough money, and can make more. Your time, effort, and skills earned you every cent of that money. You will keep it, and know you've made a customer very, very happy. I'll be sure to tell anyone who asks me where I got such a wonderful chest. And send them to see you for one of their own".

The shop keeper thanked Chase over and over again for his generosity and words of praise. Tears of joy were freely streaming down his cheeks as Chase left his shop with the chest. Chase then returned to the other shop and picked up his parcel of clothing, and hat, placed them into the chest and returned to the ship.

Once back inside his locked cabin Chase placed the chest on the small bed and opened it. He lifted out the bundle of clothing, as well as the hat, then finally the silver tray. Moving around the cabin Chase collected all the deeds he'd hidden during the voyage up to that point. When he finished collecting them all he counted them. He'd amassed sixteen deeds since beginning his trip across the ocean. He placed them into the bottom of the chest, along with his log book of names and other information.

Finally he recollected all the keys and placed them in the chest beside the stack of deeds. Thinking to himself he had been smart to of thought of labeling the keys when he first started collecting them. Otherwise by now he'd have no idea which key went to any given lock. The idea of spending periods of time working through large numbers of keys in search of the right one; was not one he wanted to have to think of again. After a few moments of thought he removed a pair of socks from the bundle of cloths and placed the keys inside one of them. Rolled it tightly closed then placed it inside of the other sock. He returned the keys to the awaiting chest, with a small sinister smile spreading across his smooth face. That would keep any from being needlessly lost, or from rattling around within the chest. Drawing unneeded attention to him or, to the chest was not something he wanted to deal with.

He then replaced the tray and neatly placed the clothing inside it. Chase left out a fresh set of cloths to put on the following day. Chase then collected and counted all the money he had collected during the voyage. He kept two hundred dollars on him and placed the remaining fifteen hundred into the chest. Once that was done he closed the chest, and locked both locks. They easily moved into place with a soft click. Chase then placed the chest in the far corner of the room away from the bed and the door. It was heavy enough that he doubted many people could easily lift it by themselves. Satisfied he emptied all his pockets onto the bed.

After ensuring all his pockets were completely empty he removed his gun belts and all his clothing. Washed himself with the cold water in the wash basin on the table. Once more glad the temperature no longer mattered to him. Chase then walked quickly around the small cabin until he was completely dry. Once he was dry he laid down on the bed. Chase enjoyed the soft breeze that came in through the small port window in the far wall as it flirted along his bare flesh, as he lay there. Chase closed his eyes and thought back over everything that had happened since getting his father's letter. Along while later he opened his eyes and sat on the side of the bed, before getting redressed in his new clothing. As he dressed he figured he would keep his old trail coat and hat for the time being. In order to save the new one for when he finally met the vampire whose blood he'd drank. He felt the ship moving back out into open water shortly after dressing. So it had been three days already. He would have to get a handle on time or he might run into problems at some point in time. An hour later he walked out on deck and casually tossed his old clothing out into the ocean. As he thought ahead to the next port, he hoped he would be able to find a suitable replacement for his currently shabby looking boots.

There were only four more stoppages after that before the ship pulled into port in Romania. Chase only left the ship during one of these stops. He wasn't going to but the woman he'd exited the ship with was boasting of owning numerous properties, loads of money, and a wine collection that none could rival. She claimed she had acquired it all when her husband had died a few years ago. Knowing the size and contents of his own personal wine collection he wanted to add hers to his. That was if it was as good as she boasted. Also his knowledge that for the remainder of his existence he would be drinking a great deal of wine fueled his desire to add to his considerable collection. As such he did not want to miss out on the chance to add her supposedly large collection to his. He also wanted to see about some new boots in case he could not find any suitable ones in Romania as he'd planned.

The old woman had been good to her word. She indeed did have a very, very large wine collection. There were also a good number of other bottled vintages such as Scotch, Rum, Rye, and other various flavors. Chase had descended upon the old lady draining her of her blood as she began to boast further of the awesome collection of bottles, just to shut the old girl up. Chase made up his mind as he let go of her lifeless body. As she crumpled to the floor at the base of a shelf full of bottles, he ensured she did not bump the shelf. Chase set his idea into action. Not wanting to leave the collection to chance in case he didn't return to this village for a long period of time, if at all. Chase took the time to package up every bottle he could find and took all the cases to the docks in a horse drawn wagon he had discovered in a large outbuilding behind his newest house. Chase found a freight vessel that was willing to take his shipment and hastily written letter back home to Gail. He knew it would boost the stock at the bar to the bursting point. That is if she had decided to keep the bar. As well as add considerably to his own private collection.

Chase found a sailor that provided him with some paper and a writing instrument, as the captain gave the required orders to his crew; to have Chase's crates loaded on the ship. Walking over to a group of wooden barrels Chase placed the paper onto one of them and quickly began to write.

> Gail,
>
> I am sending you this shipment of bottles to be stored in my basement with my wine collection (if they will fit). I had no intentions of acquiring more wine and spirits while on this trip. However this collection literally fell into my possession.
>
> I do not have the time to go through them to find out what types there are, or the values of the various different bottles. I ask that you simply put these cases with the other bottles in my basement.
>
> I pledge to you still that I am trying to complete this trip with as much haste as possible, in order to return to your loving arms faster. You are never out of my mind, and I look forward to returning to you soon.
>
> With all my Love,
> Chase

Chase had completed the letter, and had it folded inside the sole remaining blank piece of paper, before the last crate was on board the ship. Chase acquired a stick of green sealing wax from the captain, and sealed the letter closed.

Once more he used his ring to press into the seal. He knew Gail would know who it was from as soon as she seen it. Chase paid the captain his shipping fee. He also paid four of the sailors to deliver the crates to his house once the ship reached its final destination.

Between the cost of the shipping and that of the delivery, Chase had spent an additional eight hundred dollars of his money. It had actually been the original owner of the shipment's money. At least it had been before he collected it from her after draining her of her blood. Though given the size of the shipment, and what he guessed to be the value of the bottles. He thought the price was more than reasonable.

However if she had already sold the bar, or was planning on selling the bar it would almost quadruple the size of his already considerable collection. Not to mention the fact that the letter and shipment would only further add to any questions and feelings she was already dealing with in regards to him.

After quickly completing what has become a routine for him with the body, he returned to the ship. Once more alone in his locked room he added the small stack of deeds, the keys, and information to his slowly growing collection inside his chest. He then added his new boots to the chest. Having once more deciding to keep them new for when he met his mysterious blood donor. He had managed to find a shop selling suitable boots on his way back to the ship. Chase had stopped long enough to purchase a pair. After these few tasks were finished he closed and relocked the chest.

It was only two days after that, that the ship made its final stop in Romania. Chase left the ship with his chest and quickly found an inn for the night. Not wanting to travel through Romania at night, as he didn't want to miss anything. Also because it would be easier to rent a wagon during daylight hours, he would wait until daylight to go any further. Once locked inside his room, Chase lay down on the bed, closed his eyes and listened to the sounds of the strange village he was in.

As was the case in Quebec, Chase couldn't understand anything being said in the strange language of the land. Once more he was not bothered by this realization. After all he had all the time in the world thanks to his new immortal life to learn all the different languages he wanted to learn. Chase also figured he would likely be in Romania for a considerable period of time, providing his mysterious blood donor still was here. During which time he felt confident he would learn at least a working knowledge of the language.

Vladimir

Chase remained laying on the bed for the better part of the morning, taking in the sounds of the busy village. Lulled by the flow and sounds of the strange languages being spoken, from outside the thin walls. With his mind's eye Chase tried to imagine what these strange people looked like. What their clothing would look like, if it would be very different from his clothing. Chase had stayed where he was until slightly before noon. At which time he forced himself to get out of the bed, as he was slowly being lulled to sleep. And that could prove to be very dangerous, depending on who found him on the bed. If he were to fall asleep and not awaken any time soon, and being found and thought dead.

A short time later Chase was standing talking to a stable hand with his travel chest at his feet, gaining the information he desired. Chase had informed the stable hand that he needed to go to Dragomirna. As such needed to rent a wagon and horse or possibly a few horses for the journey, depending on how long it would take to make. The stable hand stated that it was almost a two week journey by wagon. As such he would not rent out a horse and wagon, unless he was to take the trip too. Otherwise Chase would have to buy them, or there was no way he would get them back. He was unsure when he could return them. As Chase had told him he was unsure of how long he was going to remain there.

Chase thought over his options for a few seconds, and then told the stable hand that he would be willing to purchase a horse and wagon, providing the price was fair. However he wanted a decent horse and a carriage or a covered wagon at the very least. Chase was offered a carriage for two hundred or a wagon for one hundred and fifty. Both with a young strong horse that could make the long journey, without issue both also with a spare horse if desired. The extra horse would cost an extra fifty dollars, if he wanted it. Chase chose the carriage, figuring it would prove to be more comfortable. It would also provide a quiet dark place to pretend to sleep if the need came up that he needed to pretend to rest. It would also give him someplace comfortable to relax while the horse rested. Whereas he could make the trip without stopping, he knew the horse would need to stop and rest at least a few hours each day.

Chase watched as the young man hitched the horse to a fair sized carriage. Chase loaded his chest into the carriage as the man finished with the last few buckles. Handing over the money, as he climbed into the padded seat at the front of the carriage, Chase asked for some directions pretending to be unfamiliar with the area, and then started on his way. At the end of the tenth day Chase finally arrived. Chase guessed he could have made the trip at least four days shorter had he not of needed to stop to rest the horse. Even though the extra time it had taken with the daily stops didn't bother him at all. It wasn't like he was short on time or anything. Other than his desire to return to Gail as fast as he possibly could.

There was also the added bonus on a few of the stops when some foolish bandits tried to rob him in the middle of the night when he was pretending to be sleeping. There lifeless bodies were easy to get rid of once he had drained them of their blood. The heavily wooded countryside of Romania held uncountable places to lose a body. With little fear that it would be found before the local wildlife had ate it. He had heard an unsettling large number of wolves every night. As the stable hand had told him, it had taken almost a full two weeks to make the journey. He suspected it would have been about a week longer than that if he had stopped to rest longer or more often than he did. It was a good thing he had been able to buy such a young, strong horse. Or he might have had no other choice but to stop for more than six hours a night.

Dragomirna turned out to be a heavily fortified building. The entire mass of it was massive; it was nearly as long as it was wide. The walls of it looked to be almost as high as the building was long. Set into the front of the building was a massive double set of doors. Judging from the size of them a pair of elephants could easily walk through them side by side. With more than enough room to spare around them easily preventing them from rubbing the sides. Chase could hear a bustle of activity coming from inside the walls. Without his vampire abilities there would have been hardly a sound at all. Chase judged that the doors were almost as thick as the walls. Which could easily be four feet thick or more.

Stopping his horse just short of the front doors, Chase dismounted from his seat. Mindful of his appearance Chase slipped inside the carriage and changed into some of his new cloths. This time he included his new hat, coat, and boots. Chase exited the carriage and looked around the area to better familiarize himself with it. Taking the few steps it took to reach the doors, Chase was just raising a hand to knock when one of the massive doors swung soundlessly open. Standing on the threshold was a fairly tall man. Chase could tell instantly that the man was also a vampire. He looked to be in his early thirties, and in good shape at the time he was turned. Chase took in his long black hair, pale complexion, and expensive clothing. The man appeared to take in his own appearance just as quickly. Chase had no idea how long the man had been a vampire. He felt to Chase to be a very old vampire, a couple hundred years old at the very least. If felt was the proper way to describe the aura the man was transmitting.

A slow fierce smile spread across the man's face.

Raising his right hand in greeting as he took a step forward, the man said, "Welcome to my humble home. I am Vladimir Von Vanpier, I assume you've come here by way of the wine".

Chase thought this was a funny statement to make. But he brushed it off quickly figuring it were some sort of localized phrasing, or due to his being an old vampire who lapsed into an ancient lingo or something.

Looking fully at the strange man in front of him Chase replied, "Yes, I have drunken deeply from your wine cache. As you can clearly see we are much the same now. I have come seeking answers, as you claimed to be able to educate me on my new lifestyle. I truly hope you will answer my questions without feeling overly pestered by me, as I have scores of them".

Vladimir laughed and said, "All in due time my son. First come inside, and I'll make you at home. After which I will answer all your questions and majority of the ones you haven't thought of yet".

With that said the second huge door swung open. Vladimir motioned to the horse, and it walked to him. Taking up the reins in his strong left hand, he turned and walked back through the open doors, with Chase walking along beside him. Now that was a trick that Chase would need to learn. It could come in very handy at some point he reasoned.

When the back of the carriage passed inside the doors they slowly closed seemingly by themselves. Chase stopped and looked longingly back at the doors. Hoping to catch a look at who had opened and closed them. However no one was near them.

Knowing what he was thinking Vladimir said, "You will notice a lot of strange things happening within these old walls. During your time here though you will come to understand them, I am sure. Then they will become less strange to you, and make more sense".

Looking around Chase soon realized that the long high walls were more of an illusion, than a reality. From the outside they made the place look like a huge heavily fortified building. In actuality they served more as a fortification for several smaller buildings hidden inside of them. Vladimir explained as they went deeper into the keep that Dragomirna actually housed twenty five buildings on the surface. And a huge three level subterranean vault, which was also contained within the parameters of the outer walls. Which he also stated fortified the outer walls of the vault, as they extended far below the surface as well.

They stopped in front of the largest building a short time later. Vladimir informed Chase that it was where he lived. And that it also housed the only access point to the vault below ground. Smiling broadly Vladimir stated that even if any would be thief be lucky enough to make it into his house, they would never find nor open the entrance to the hidden vault below. The entrance is very well hidden, and totally undetectable without any prior knowledge of it. Or with far more than a boat load of luck and a lot of hard work. They walked past the house a few minutes later to a slightly smaller house, and stopped once more. Vladimir further informed Chase that it had once been an infirmary during a long forgotten little war; however it had been empty for a little over a century. Vladimir told Chase to go into the building and make himself at home. Vladimir informed

Chase that from then on whenever he stopped in Romania in the future; the house would be his. As such he was free to do with it as he would. Also that if need be anything that he left within its walls would be touched by none save Chase himself. Regardless how long he chose to leave whatever it was there.

Chase was to find him at his house later once he was settled. Chase was then informed there was a stable behind the house where his horse and carriage would be housed for him. Barely had the words exited Vladimir's mouth when a slim old man all but materialized beside him and deftly plucked the horse's reins out of his hand. Vladimir introduced the old man simply as Carter, and informed Chase he would be his personal stable hand. As such the stable was also his as an extension of the house. Vladimir urged Chase to collect his belongings from the carriage, assuring him that Carter would attend to everything else. Chase took his chest from within the carriage and entered the house for the first time. Once inside Chase set down the chest inside the front door. He turned around to say something further but Vladimir was already gone. After which he wandered from room to room. Taking in the entire house and its' layout.

Although Vladimir has claimed the house had been empty for over a century. It had been updated and renovated though out the years. It smelled of new wood, plaster, and paint. There was a large sitting room just inside the front door, and to the left. On the opposite side was a large den or small library depending on how you felt like terming it, as it could serve as either. With its current appearance, the modest furnishings and two walls of floor to ceiling book shelves, which were already full of books. Chase found himself already thinking of it as a library and not a den. Following the wide long hallway deeper into the house, his thoughts drifted. Chase discovered a massive kitchen on the left just past a pair of staircases. The stairs on the left lead up, while the ones on the right lead down.

Opposite the kitchen was a large dining room, and medium sized storage room. Running across the back of the house, with access from the kitchen was a massive cold storage room and pantry. Thinking as the vampire he now was he considered all this kitchen and storage area little more than wasted space. He knew as a vampire he had no need to store or prepare human food.

Following the hallway back towards the front of the house Chase took the staircase leading upwards. A long wide hallway stretched out the length of the house. There were three doors on either side accenting the distance down the hall. Opening each one as he traveled further and further down the hallway and looking inside. In order to determine what lay hidden behind each one of them. Behind each was a large bedroom. The furniture within the last room on the right hand side appealed to him the most, so Chase mentally chose this room for himself. Each bedroom was massive. Each one was the size of a little apartment, than the size of a mere bedroom. Each had its own bathroom and walk-in closets.

Chase returned to the main floor, he then took the other staircase downwards. At the very bottom of the stairs Chase discovered a large heavy wooden door. Lifting the ancient latch and pushing against it gently, caused it to freely swing open. Behind which was a single room, which housed rows upon rows of shelves. Every shelf was filled to spilling with bottles of wine. There had to be at least six thousand bottles housed in the massive room. Smiling to himself Chase chose a bottle from the nearest shelf.

Smiling more broadly, ah he thought to himself, "I think I'm going to like it here".

He slowly walked back to the kitchen.

He reflected on how his entire life had been so remarkably changed with what appeared to be no more than a mere bottle of old wine. Chase realized for the first time that since his transformation he had developed a new fondness for wine. Remembering a time not so distant when he knew such a cache of wine would have turned his stomach.

Chase opened the bottle of wine, before setting it on the counter to "air". Taking the time to take his chest up to the room he'd chosen for himself. After quickly unpacking his few cloths, he relocked the chest. With all the deeds, keys and his money locked safely inside. Even though he was told the house was his. He still did not feel entirely comfortable in it. Chase returned to the kitchen to enjoy the bottle of wine. Chase easily found a heavy cut crystal goblet in one of the many cupboards. Pouring himself a glass of wine, he turned towards the front of the house and went to the living room with the glass of wine. He placed the remainder of the bottle on the small side table.

Chase sat on the sofa slowly drinking the flavorful wine, as he put his thoughts in order. Gail was on the forefront of his mind. He couldn't help but wonder what she was doing, or if she had forgiven him. Though there was no way for him to know or find out from where he was. As such he pushed the thoughts further back into his mind. Although with a great deal of more difficulty than he would ever admit too. For the first time he realized just how much he actually missed her. And to be completely honest with himself he couldn't even say how long it had been since he had last seen her. Even though in his mind's eye it was only yesterday. Still his heart ached for her to be at his side once more.

Chase made a vow to finish in Romania as quickly as he could so he could return to her side, if she wanted him there.

Which he fiercely hoped that she did, especially given his own failure to keep her out of his mind. Chase finished off the bottle of wine, before figuring it was time to track Vladimir down. Judging enough time had passed for him not to appear too eager for answers. Armed with a good number of questions Chase strolled over the house Vladimir stated was his.

Chase seen a number of other people moving around the grounds as he walked next door, some of them stopped and looked towards him, however majority of them went about their business, without so much as a glance in his direction. When Chase reached the front door, it opened before he could raise his hand to knock, just as the door to the keep had done when he arrived. From deep within he heard Vladimir telling him to enter and make himself at home. Chase walked into the richly decorated home and stopped short in awe. Never before had he seen such a stunning display of wealth.

The large door behind him swung soundlessly closed. If not for the change in the air flow, he never would have noticed the door had been closed. Chase walked further into the house and into the first doorway on his left. It was a large darkly paneled room. A low fire was burning in the huge fireplace on the opposite side of the room. Flanking either side were floor to ceiling bookshelves, crammed to their limits with books.

There were two large sofas and three high back arm chairs arranged tastefully in front of the fireplace in a semi-circle. A long wide coffee table closed the distance of the arch they created. Standing under the rooms' only window was a formidable looking table. A large number of loose pages were covering majority of the surface. Chase crossed the wide floor and sat down on one of the large sofas.

A short time passed before Vladimir joined Chase in the room. Chase never heard him enter the room, nor cross the floor.

Chase was staring into the fire thinking, and the next thing he knew Vladimir was sitting on the other sofa looking at him. When Chase minutely started and turned his head to look full at him. Vladimir settled back into the sofa with a wry smile spread across his face.

After looking each other over for a few minutes Vladimir said, "You certainly look to be in good health. Obviously you have been feeding, and feeding well at that. You must tell me your story from the beginning to the end. Make sure to include every detail, so I will know what I need to educate you on. Depending on how long it's been since you drank my wine and what you've learned on your own, how much I will need to teach you. There is no sense wasting time trying to teach you what you already know".

This made perfect sense to Chase. However by the time he had finished telling his entire story at least three days had passed that he was aware of. It surprised him that he had that much to tell. To him it seemed like only a few days had passed since he'd drunk the wine. It also surprised him that the entire time he had been talking no one had disturbed them. Truth be told so did the fact that neither one of them had moved at all during the entire time, nor felt the need to take a break to rest.

When he had finally finished talking Vladimir said, "You have learned a great deal in the short time that you have been a vampire. You are a quick learner, therefore it won't take you long to learn what I have to teach you. However I think our conversation has gone on for long enough for the time being. If we stay held up within these walls very much longer, someone is bound to come looking for me. So I propose we leave things off here for now and get back together tomorrow morning. At which time I'll answer your questions".

Chase agreed with the idea, as he was beginning to feel hungry. Vladimir walked him to the front door, and bid him farewell for the time being. Chase wandered around the inside of the walls of the keep. Familiarizing himself with the layout, and admiring the buildings. As he wandered he stopped and talked to a number of people. Surprisingly they were all very friendly. He was able to identify who was a vampire easily even before getting close to them. However majority of the people he seen and talked to appeared to be humans. Some of them had a feel to them that Chase could not describe. For lack of a better term they felt to be "more" than human. Not that he could describe just how, nor why he felt this way about them.

Chase made a mental note to himself to find out how so many humans could live within the walls. None of which seemed to realize or care that they were mingling with vampires. Could they be that oblivious, or was there another reason. He was determined to find out tomorrow, when he resumed his conversation with Vladimir. He vowed to himself to leave them all unharmed as he did not want to anger his host. With that thought firmly in mind he headed back to the house, he was using. It was time to find something to eat. Back inside the house he headed for the kitchen; to see what was there he could eat.

To his surprise there were a large number of containers in the cupboard. That has not been there when he looked in them before he was sure of it. They all looked to be full of blood. He pulled one out and opened it. The sharp slightly metallic scent of blood accosted him. His stomach rumbled. Raising the glass jar up he smelled it before putting it to his lips, the smell of blood made his stomach lurch again. Chase drank it down greedily. With a few quick swallows the jar was empty. It wasn't nearly as good as blood fresh from a body. Though it would do the trick for the time being at least…although it was close. He could tell it had been harvested while the donor had been alive. It tasted nothing like the blood he had tried to drink from his two would be robbers. So it couldn't have come from a dead body.

Chase went through the motions over and over again, until he could drink no more. By the time he was done there were two dozen empty bottles on the counter top. Chase figured that he had drunk enough blood to have drained six people. It was a great lesson on the importance of having a backup supply on hand. He would have to figure out a way to ensure he had a ready supply of his own. He planned to ask Vladimir if he had any suggestions to this end, when they got back together to resume their talk. It was clear he could drain a body for later use. However there were now more questions than answers. Like how long the blood could be stored before it was undrinkable. Chase felt this was the most important question to have answered.

Chase returned to the room he'd planned to stay in the first night and washed up, and dressed in fresh clothing. After which he found some books that looked interesting and sat to read. By the time morning arrived he had finished reading four books from cover to cover. An impressive feat on its own, seeing as he'd never finished a single book in his human life. Laying the finished books aside, he decided it was time to return to Vladimir to continue their conversation.

Andy Elliott

Enlightenment

Vladimir met Chase at the door when he walked towards the house. After a short greeting they returned to the room they left the night before. Once they resumed their positions on their respective sofas, Vladimir began to speak. He began by telling Chase of when and how he had become a vampire. Glossing over a great deal of the details to keep the story short and because he'd already shared some of it in the book with the wine.

Still countless hours had passed during his narrative.

When he had finished, he said, "Enough about me. You've got a lot of questions; I've got the answers to them. From our previous conversation I know you want to be on your way back to where you came from as soon as you can. So sit back and relax, I'll tell you what you need to know, and what I think you want to know. When I'm done if you've still questions I haven't answered, you can ask them then".

When Chase agreed and sat back more comfortably on the sofa, Vladimir began speaking once more. "As I briefly told you in the book I left with my wine. There are a great many things I can tell you about being a vampire. However in order to tell you everything I know, it would take me years to do so. As your wishing for our time together at present to be as short as possible. I'll merely give you the shortest version I can, merely covering the most important things.

Vampires are not the only creatures in the world. Along-side of us there is also witches and daemons. Humans acknowledge us, but tell themselves we are not real. They commonly refer to daemons as demons. In your travels here you've already met at least one witch. From your description of her "feel' and "smell", I feel confident in assuring to you that Dawn is a witch. And a very powerful one at that, based upon your description of her.

It is surprising to me however that she stayed in your company for as long as she did. Majority of witches keep a distance from our kind. As do daemons. However the reason and explanation for this is long and best left for another time. It is enough to say that over time you will learn to tell whether someone you encounter is human, vampire, witch or daemon. Their feel and smell will alert you as to which race they belong to. I'm sure you have noticed scores of people milling about within the walls of this keep. Whereas a good number of them are vampire's as I am sure you can tell. A good number of them are witches and daemons as well. Before you leave my company I will educate you on which race they belong to. By the time we are done you will be able to pick out each race from a fair distance away.

I know I said they usually keep a distance from us. But the longer you live and the more we talk, the general rule will become little more than a blurred line. Again as it is a long story I will not tell it to you now. There are also a small number of humans living here. They also have some use and purposes to us. However I will caution you to be very, very careful of which one's you decide to allow close to you, if any at all. Take your time to learn as much about them as you can, before taking them into your homes. Trust me on this, I only tell you this for your own safety.

There are also ghosts present all around us. They generally are more common in places where witches live and spend majority of their time. But that does not mean you will not find them in other places from time to time. It goes without saying that in areas where large numbers of people have died there is equally large numbers of ghosts. Wars are really nothing more than breading grounds for scores of them. Although not all people who die become ghosts, a good number of them will…but not all of them. The closest I've been able to figure it out is. If a person is not ready to die they become a ghost or if their lives ended unexpectedly. I have a number of them living right here in my house for instance. More which that live right here within the walls of this very keep. They are the ones who have been opening and closing the doors. Ah, Chase thought that explains it. No wonder he couldn't see anyone opening or closing the door. So much for it being a vampire trick.

However we are all family here, as such every creature within the outer walls are under my full protection. In time you may come to know other covens. For that is what we vampires call a collection of people living together. However few are as big as this one is. You may also at some point decide you want to form your own coven. I caution you to speak further and more in depth with me first, before making this choice. Trust me on this I've very good reasons for saying this. Which I will not go into detail of at this time, as that conversation alone would take a great deal of time.

It is of the utmost importance for you to choose where you will live at any given time throughout your existence with great care. Whereas humans try to pretend we do not exist. From time to time some have had a tendency, to go too far and attempt to track and kill us. We can be killed, but it is not an easy thing to do. Our bodies would have to be greatly damaged. So much so that we lose a great deal of blood quickly, rendering our abilities to heal ourselves far too slow to compensate with the blood leaving our bodies; which would cause us to bled out and die.

As I'm sure you have heard fire will destroy us. Due to our nature if we are exposed to flame our bodies ignite like a pile of dry tinder. Though to be perfectly honest I have heard rumors of some of our kind that were powerful enough to even withstand fire. But I have to admit in all my years I have not met any. If for some reason your head is separated from the rest of your body, providing your body stays otherwise intact, you will survive. However I have only seen this once for myself, and the head was reunited with the body within minutes. I have no way of knowing with any certainty that we could live through a long term separation of such.

I do know however if our heart were to be removed from our chests we die. Even though our hearts do not beat unless we will them too, and concentrate on the task of keeping it beating. Other than those few examples we are truly immortal and will outlive the other creatures on this planet for countless years to come.

To expel some of the myths you might have heard about us. Religious items, including buildings do not weaken nor destroy us. We can hold, or be near a cross for instance with no issues what so ever. We can enter a church at any time during the day or night, even during a religious service. The only reason that might prevent us is our heightened hearing. The amplified sounds within the churches are very hard on the ears. Some of our kind had already been driven insane due to prolonged forced exposure within these places.

Our bodies can process small amount of human food at a time. Majority of foods taste like ash to us, but we can eat them. Just as when you were human, you had preferred foods. So will you now, albeit they will doubtlessly have changed. Personally I find raw meats, fresh berries and fruits, as well as most types of nuts appealing. However that does not necessarily mean you will enjoy the same things I do. That being said, I have never met one of our kind that did not enjoy wine. Usually red wine, but again it comes down to personal taste. My personal tastes for wine lean more towards vintages over one hundred years old, and are sweet and fruity tasting.

If you have not taken the time to fully explore the house I gave you. You will find a very well stocked wine pantry within your basement".

At this Chase smiled and confessed that he had already found, and sampled from the huge wine collection housed in his basement. Chase asked Vladimir if it was a vamperic appeal to wine that swayed him to make his own personal brand, which thus was the reason Chase was talking to him in the first place. Or if it was a mere trick someone else had impressed upon him as he had Chase.

Vladimir confessed that even when he had been mortal he had an affliction for wine. Since his becoming a vampire himself had only intensified his desire for it.

Smiling Vladimir said, "I figured my special wine would be safe from people who did not like wine. Or decided to heed the warnings I left in my journal with the bottles.

Sunlight will not destroy us, even direct sunlight. We can wander around day in and day out, without getting so much as a tan. As I'm sure from your tale of coming here referred to, you already know. Although you didn't come right out and say; you seem the type to test your limits, as am I. I doubt you could have traveled with your witch friend for as long as you did, solely at night.

The only reason our kind are not found out in it more is because it makes us stand out. It can be increasingly difficult to blend in with humans in direct sunlight. Especially if you have not fed for a long period of time; we tend to stand out even more.

Or if a large number of non-human creatures gather together in one place, even witches for that matter as they ARE human. Find it hard to blend in within large groups of our kind. Dim or low light make us appear less pale and otherworldly. Even then it is important to proceed with caution. Humans can and often prove to be unpredictable. Some believing rumors they have heard will attempt to seek us out with hope of becoming one of us. Most of us don't make fledglings without a great deal of thought or to us a very good reason. Some of our kind have never or will never make a single fledgling.

We do not need to feed every night as you have no doubt figured out by now. Depending on what you are doing how often you will need to feed. The more you exert yourself the faster your body absorbs the blood within you, and you will need to feed to replenish it. Likewise if your body becomes damaged you will require more blood to heal it. The greater the damage, the more blood needed. Just remember if your body is too greatly damaged, you will die for good before it will be able to heal itself. Regardless of how old or powerful you may become.

Running or fresh open water or for that matter holy water does not harm us. As I'm sure you found out we can cross large bodies of water whenever we choose too. We are excellent swimmers as we do not tire easily, and we do not need to breath. Anyone of our kind could easily swim across the widest body of water in the world, without issue. However crossing water is simply easier by boat, as it allows us to bring items with us. Not to mention it would be very hard to explain what we were doing should we become discovered swimming in the middle of an ocean for example.

We cannot change shape or form. We cannot turn into mist, nor bats. Also we cannot fly. Though we can move at great rates of speed, which can make it appear as if we are flying. Fire can destroy our bodies, as I have already told you. However it would have to be very hot, and consume our body sufficiently enough to prevent it from healing fast enough to reverse the damage done to it. Sticking your hand into the flame of a candle for instance would do little more than damage your hand. Providing your skin did not ignite. Although even that damage would heal itself in a short period of time, once the hand was away from the flame; and enough fresh blood drank. Or you have a sufficient supply of blood in your body. Though it can be a painful process to endure, as we do feel pain; albeit a great deal of pain is required for us to feel it; fledglings like you feel far more than I would. However if your entire body is consumed within flames you will be nothing more than a pile of ashes on the floor within seconds. So would my very own body.

We possess great amounts of strength. Can amass great deals of wealth if we put our minds to it, if we so desire. I caution you to be mindful of human currency as it does change from time to time. Gold, Silver, or other things of great value such as diamonds are a better way to increase your worth, without having to update with the times. Maybe in the future there will be easier ways to amass money without needing to change it to the modern currency. However we have not made it there as of yet, but one must stay hopeful".

It became obvious to Chase that Vladimir had been in isolation from the rest of the world for quite some time as he was ignorant to the recent invention of banks. Whereas they were very new still, they would be perfect for storing mass amounts of money. Leaving one free to access it whenever they wanted to, and in the current form of currency when they withdrawal it.

Chase took the time to inform Vladimir about banks and how they worked. With a sheepish smile Vladimir admitted that he had not left his safe haven for almost one hundred years, and was thus behind the times indeed. Vladimir assured him that he would look into finding the closest bank and deposit his own vast fortune into it. As he was getting tired of having to constantly, or so it seemed, of modernizing it, in order to continue using it when he desired to. Vladimir also informed Chase that because he had seen fit to share this valuable information with him, he would also be opening an account in Chase's name and depositing a considerable amount into it as a thank you gift. Chase attempted to talk him out of it, with no luck.

It is also very important to change our identities every thirty or forty years. This also will help us blend in and appear more human. There are many tricks and methods of doing this. Over time you will find a way that works best for you. Whether it be by moving or assuming a different identity. That is providing you want to be a part of the human world, and don't decide to take a break from it as I have.

For now that will serve for a short introduction to our kind. There are a great many other things I can tell you, and teach you. However none of them are overly pressing. I think that, that should answer majority of your questions for the time being. Other things you will either figure out on your own, or you can rejoin me sometime in the future and I can share the information with you then. There is only one other thing I need to share with you for the time being that cannot be put off".

Vladimir became very ridged and somber before pressing on, "There are certain rules all vampires must follow. Failure to do so will result in being hunted down and destroyed. By breaking any of these rules you will find it impossible to go anywhere or hide any place. There are vampires in the world far older and more powerful than I am. As such they have the abilities to find any one of our kind, and destroy them. In fact there is a vampire council to enforce the rules. The rules are very simple and easy to remember.

DO NOT DO ANYTHING TO ALLOW HUMANS TO KNOW WE ACTUALLY EXIST. Meaning hide or disguise all your kills. Don't ever go on a killing spree, unless it can easily be disguised as something else. For example during wars, or revolutions it is easier to hide dead bodies DO NOT OPENLY ENTER INTO HOSTILITIES AMOUNG OUR KIND, UNLESS IT IS JUSTIFIABLE. For example another vampire enters into your territory without your permission. As such do not enter into another vampires territory knowingly without their permission, or letting them know as soon as you find out it is their territory.

If unsure contact me and I'll let you know if and who a given vampire is in a given territory. For the time being you are the only vampire in the area where you come from. As far as I know there is only one other vampire in Canada. Though she is in the far northern hemisphere, and does not venture south very often. Although when she learns of another vampire living in Canada she may feel the need to visit you. She is about a thousand years older than I am, so if she decided to visit, you should show her a great deal of respect. She is a very powerful vampire.

Before you leave my company I will provide you with a detailed list of the vampires and their respective territories. Though I will caution you some of the names may have changed over the past hundred years, and I am thus unaware. I will also provide you with a brief written outline of the current process of entering or passing through another vampire's territory. On the bright side not every vampire has a territory. That right is reserved solely for master vampires. A vampire rises to master status once he or she gains a high enough power level. Though not all powerful vampires will become masters either; some simply don't want the responsibility. But once again this in itself is a very long conversation, so I will leave it for another time.

DO NOT OPENLY KILL ANOTHER VAMPIRE, UNLESS THEY HAVE EARNED THE DEATH BY WRONGING YOU OR BREAKING A RULE. Either way just make sure you have proof of why they needed to die. This will protect you from the vampire counsel, and prevent them from hunting you down and killing you.

Your best bet is to petition the council before taking matters into your own hands, at least until you learn how they view things, and become a stronger vampire yourself.

With age come's more power, abilities, and strength. The longer you live the stronger you will be. However there are no pre-determine increments of time to determine if or when you will gain abilities. Some vampires live thousands of years and never gain any additional abilities. The same can be said of master vampire's. And before you ask, no there is no way to know who will become a master vampire and who will not. Although some bloodlines do have a tendency to produce more masters than others. As you are my first fledgling, at least that I know of, I have no idea if my bloodline is one of them. That being said by drinking from my blood you are already stronger than some fledglings. As such if you decide to make fledglings of your own they will also be stronger as a direct result. This is due to my vamperic age and power level when I made my wine.

As you have learned a human can be turned into a vampire by drinking wine mixed with our blood. By the way you will need to refill the bottles you emptied in my chest, and replace it where you found it. Or some other hiding place of your choice once you find one, as you are now the owner of it. To do so mix half a bottle of your blood with half a bottle of wine, and then seal it shut. I only ask that in doing so you choose a good quality wine to mix with your blood, as I did. For a fine wine is only fitting for such fine blood.

You can also turn a human into a vampire by draining their blood into you, up to the point their heart is about to stop. Then and only then, have them drink your blood from your body. However this way the change will be more violent for them, and you have to stop them from feeding on you before they drain you completely. I think that should pretty much prepare you for your new life as a vampire. Do you have any questions left that I have not answered for you already?".

Chase confirmed that he did not have anything left he could think of that needed answers right away. He thanked Vladimir for all the knowledge he'd shared. As it was closing in on twilight Chase took up the offer for him to spend the rest of the evening within the outer walls. As it was too clear to Vladimir that now that Chase had the answers to his questions, he wanted to be away.

Chase spent the remained of the evening held up in the house he was given. The night drug by ever so slowly. Chase suspected that it seemed that way as he wanted to leave as soon as darkness fell. However stopped himself from doing so only because he didn't know the area well enough to travel it at night. He didn't want to end up lost and spend more time away from Gail as a result of it. As soon as the sun began to rise, he would be on his way. Chase left the house to get his horse and carriage from the stables, he found during his wandering, to be just behind his house as Vladimir had told him it was.

Once he had hitched the horse to the carriage he led it back to the house. Loaded his chest back inside of it, then went back next door to let Vladimir know he was leaving. Vladimir walked him to the huge doors set into the outer walls of the keep. After a short goodbye, and open invitations to each other Chase departed heading for what had once again become his home.

In the essence of speed, Chase hired a private ship to carry him back across the water. There were a large number of boats willing to make the voyage. As a result it cost him half of what it did to get to Romania.

Chase kept the horse and carriage with him, to add some speed to his return home. As a result he arrived back home in a mere three months from the time he had set sail from Romania. It was difficult to admit that he had been away for a little over five and a half years. Even though he felt as if he had only been gone for a couple of months, even he knew it had been far longer. He was happier than he thought would be possible when he once more seen what had been his father's old house. Putting the chest inside it, and tethering the horse to the back porch, Chase figured it was time to seek out Gail's response. He hoped it would be in his favor, though feared it as well. He didn't know how she would handle the truth. And he didn't want to have to kill her if she took it badly.

Chase walked around to the front of his house. Opened up the front door and walked back inside. Searching the piles of mail, he did not find anything from Gail. Especially not the key he had left with her. Though he could see with his keen eyes that the living room was now packed full with the crates he had shipped home. Taking that for a sign of luck Chase set out for her house. He couldn't wait a minute longer to find out if she's hung the slip of blue fabric in an upstairs window. Part way to her house he had another thought.

Chase stopped and turned back towards home. He walked inside and straight upstairs to the den.

Sitting down at his late father's old desk he wrote a quick note for Gail. It read, *"I was able to see the blue fabric clearly. I am home come see me when you want to. Use your key to let yourself in".*

Once this was completed he once more set out for Gail's house. As he turned onto her street the sun was just rising off in the distance. He stopped long enough to watch it climb above the furthest trees he could see. He had always enjoyed watching the sun rise.

Something In Blue

Half a block down the street from Gail's house Chase could see that it had changed. The entire house had been painted a light blue color. In each and every window there hung either blue curtains or blue blinds of some form. Laughing to himself and smiling like a lunatic Chase realized this was Gail's answer. There was no way he could mistaken her answer. She wanted him back in her life. Chase felt like an ass for even thinking that she wouldn't want him back. Even though he had briefly re-entered her life only to just as quickly disappear for it again, or so it must have seemed to her.

Remembering that Gail was an early riser Chase quickly closed the distance to the house. Silently he crept up onto the porch and placed his note on the door knob, where it would flutter to the floorboards when she opened the door. He quickly retreated back up the street. When he heard her get out of bed, his feet had barely made it to the gutter. Maybe he had gotten it all wrong. When he put the note on her door knob, Chase could have sworn he had heard three different heart beats in Gail's house. Had she actually found someone else and started a life with them?

He was standing in some shadows under a maple tree at the top of the street, watching as her front door opened. He watched her bend down and pick up his note, a mere second after it touched the floorboards. He watched as Gail looked down at the note. A second later her head jerked up and she let out a gasp of air.

Judging he didn't have much time he quickly headed back home. Due to his vampire speed he was home again in less than a minute. By the early morning light that was slightly spilling in through the front windows. Chase set the chest of Immortal Wine on the coffee table in the front room, and sat on the couch furthest from the doorway into the room. After first making room in the room by moving majority of the cases of wine he shipped to Gail into the dinning room. He was cloaked in shadows, half hidden from sight. When he heard Gail walk up onto the front porch and enter the house, ten minutes later.

Admitting to himself her key sent the ghost of a chill along his spine when she turned it, forcing the lock to spring open. He settled more fully back onto the couch, deeper into the shadows when she walked inside the house. The old sofa made a slight squeak of protest when he moved. He had been counting on the noise to give away his presence and location.

Which it was apparent that it did, as Gail stopped outside of the living room doorway and asked, "Chase are you in here?"

Smiling to himself Chase replied, "I'm in here sitting on the sofa Gail, Please come on in and join me".

Gail slowly walked into the room, to give her eye's time to adjust to the low light spilling in the window. Half way into the room she was barely able to see Chase sitting on the sofa.

She stopped behind the chair facing him and said, "Your all in shadow, let's turn on some light so I can see you better".

Sitting up straighter on the sofa Chase said to her, "Let's leave the lighting as it is for now. We need to talk and I don't want to distract you with how much I've changed since last you've seen me. I know I owe you a lot of explanations, if you'll sit a while I'd like to give them to you now".

Gail walked around the chair and lowered herself into it before responding with, "I don't know what all the mystery is all about. However if this is the way you want it fine. I'm just happy that you are back, and don't want to risk losing you again. There are things I need to share with you as well".

Gail sat silently wringing her hands together in her lap as her eye's continued to adjust to the poor lighting.

After what seemed to her like an eternity had passed, Chase finally said to her, 'I'll let you tell me first what it is you wish to, for I know what I have to tell you will take far longer to tell. Please go on, and then I'll tell you my tale".

Thinking it a strangely formal way to say what he did Gail gathered her resolve and began, "The night you returned and we re-met, was one of the happiest in my life. Sure I probably drank too much of the wine, and acted a little loosely. However I do not take back my actions. I am happy we made love to each other throughout the night and into the morning. I still blush when I think of how it made me feel when you were buried deep inside me. I think it is only fair to tell you, you are only the second man I've ever been to bed with, in my life. But you're the only one who I have ever truly loved.

Then I left you alone for the day so I could go to work. When I came back you were obsessed with that book you found with all that wine. I could tell even though you never said so, nor would be likely to admit it even now. Not wanting to seem too clingy I figured I would give you the time to read it in peace, so I left you and returned home. I figured you would have come calling on me a few hours later, or the next day at the latest. Then you disappeared from my life, without a single word. I was heartbroken, I really thought we had entered into a relationship, but was crushed when I didn't hear from you after that day. That was why I wrote you that letter and left it on your porch. I had no idea if you would even get it, or read it if you did.

Then a couple days after I left it I got your letter. I was over the moon with joy. It took me a long time to understand why you were leaving me so quickly. Though I read your letter a number of times trying to make sense of it all. I was mad at you for leaving me like that. I almost tore your letter up, along with the deed to the bar. But after a long hard cry, I tried to see things through your eyes.

I'd figured I'd act strangely and do apparently strange things too if I'd just lost my father and step-mother the way that you did. I began to think that in time you might come back to me. I took your advice and quite my job and re-opened the bar. Oh and in case you are still wondering I had been working at the bank for the previous five years as a teller. The bar is a good business, and I've now got good people working there and running it for me. It makes a good deal of money, providing it keeps doing well I'll be comfortable for the rest of my life. That is unless you want it back now that you have returned.

I think it was two weeks after I received your letter that I did all of that, sorry I stayed mad at you for so long but I really was heartbroken. It was around the same time that I put up the blue blinds. I wanted to make sure you could see them so I put them in all of my windows. After a couple of weeks I paid someone to paint the house blue, also to ensure you knew I wanted you in my life. I didn't want you to miss that message. Though I went through all those changes, I wasn't done as I later found out".

There was a message painted on Gail's face as she said this. However even with his vampire powers Chase had no idea what it could be.

"That night and morning we made more than just love and happy memories. Chase I was as I later found out, pregnant with your baby. I only realized I was with child a week or so after painting the house. Being as inexperienced in coupling as I am it took me longer than it should have to realize the changes in my body. I gave birth to our son nine months later. As I was unsure by that time if you were going to return or not I named him Chase Junior in honor of you. With re-opening the bar I had enough money to hire a live-in nanny for him.

She has been a god's send. Mackayla is her name; she is with Chase Junior now. I woke her before I left. I told her I would be here, and it may take me some time to return. I also told her to come find me here if she needed anything, I hope that was ok. I want you in my life now and forever. I want us to have a happy family and watch our child grow up together. Please tell me that you feel the same way".

When Gail finished speaking Chase could only sit and stare at her for a long time. What she said took a while to fully sink in and even longer to fully process. On one hand he was over the moon with joy himself, that she had gave birth to his child. On the other hand it only made all that he had to tell her even more difficult. He needed time to think, unfortunately looking at her sitting across from him; he knew she would not leave him again without some explanations first.

Looking at her smiling Chase finally said, "Well that is a lot to process. Let me start by saying I never wanted to hurt you, or be away from you once we were together again after so many years. I gave you the bar, and I meant it when I said I wanted you to keep it. I love you too, and have for as long as I can remember. I'm going to be…no, I am a father, wow, now that is awesome. Unfortunately it makes what I need to tell you all the harder. However before you even think it, I'm not going anywhere ever again without you, unless you change your mind about wanting me in your life.

I'm torn now though, I want to tell you everything. However after what you just told me it changes everything again. I need time to think, but I don't want you to think you scared me off or that I'm going to disappear on you or our son. Can you wait here for a few minutes while I go down stairs and get a bottle of wine?"

When she didn't answer for a few minutes Chase added, "With that news we need to celebrate, our son's life and our new life together. As my sorted tale and our good fortune are all due to a bottle of old wine. I think a fine bottle of wine would only be fitting for us to share while celebrating our son".

With tears of joy silently tracing lines down her checks Gail smiled at Chase and said, "I'll wait here for as long as it takes you to return to me. I only ask that you return to me, sooner rather than later".

Chase got up from the sofa and went to the basement for a bottle of wine. He took longer than he needed to get one. As he'd picked up the first really old looking bottle he found. A few minutes later his quick mind had come to what he hope would be the best course of action for him to take.

Chase walked slowly back upstairs into the kitchen. A full five minutes after he left to get the wine he returned to the living room with the open bottle of wine and two glasses. Sitting on the edge of the sofa he poured them both a full glass of the wine. Set the bottle down in the middle of the table beside the second glass, and sat back fully onto the sofa.

After taking a long slow sip of the wine he said, "I wasn't sure if you'd want some too, as I forgot to ask you before. I brought you a glass though in case you do want some".

It is fine if you do not, I will drink that glass for you if you don't.

Laughing slightly Gail replied, "As I can now celebrate your return, and the birth of our son with you, I would not pass up the chance for the entire world".

Gail picked up the second glass, and then took a long slow drink from it. Watching Chase's lean face the entire time trying to read his thoughts; and failing to very badly. Nodding in bewildered agreement Chase took another sip of his wine. Looking into Gail's eye's as he swallowed the wine, Chase figured he had better tell her something.

With an easy smile spreading across his face Chase said, "In light of what you just shared with me, and of what I have to share with you. I'd like you to do something for me if you will".

Gail murmured that she would do anything for him. Putting down his wine glass Chase retrieved the key from its hidden drawer and opened the chest in front of him. Smiling at Gail across the chest he reached inside and took out the book. Holding it in one hand he reclosed the chest and relocked it, as Gail watched in silence. Placing the book on his lap with his hands folded lightly on top of it, Chase sat back once more.

He could easily hear Gail's heart hammering away quickly in her chest.

He counted twenty beats before he began to speak, "Gail I have a lot to tell you. Some of it will make no sense at first. Some of it will sound too fantastic to be true. Just as some of it will no doubt scare you some. I love and respect you too much to keep anything from you. I know that after I tell you what I have to tell you, you may not ever want to see me again. I will confess now that some of my story I will keep from you…at least for now. If at some point in the future you want to hear the rest. I will tell it to you. But for the time being I think it would only serve to make things more difficult so I shall keep it to myself.

Then again you might surprise me once more. As I told you earlier I need time to think, and get my thoughts in order. So if you're willing I would like you to take this book and read it. I'll freshen up one of the bedrooms upstairs for you. You can stay here while you read the book. It will serve as a great beginning to my tale. As this little book actually is the beginning of my tale. Once you have read it, part of what I have to tell you will make more sense. When you have finished reading the book you will find me in my bedroom. By that time I'll be ready to tell you the rest of my tale".

Gail thought this was an acceptable plan.

To Chase she said, "I'll read your book even though I can't imagine what it has to do with anything. It might take me a while to read it, as truth be known I'm not very good at reading. But I will read it from cover to cover none the less. Then I will look for you in your bedroom as you have asked. But just to be clear Chase, nothing you have to tell me could possibly scare me away from you. You are irreversibly stuck with me from now on".

Chase asked Gail if she needed time to go home and let Mackayla know she would be here for longer than she had originally planned. Gail assured him that Mackayla would be fine with Chase Junior until she returned however long it took. If anything important came up she would come find her.

With those arrangements made Chase left Gail briefly to prepare the bedroom for her. Once upstairs he decided to put her back in the room she had briefly used the night she'd stayed over before joining him in his bed. He quickly freshened up the bed. Fetched her a clean glass and a large pitcher of cold water, in case she got thirsty. Almost as an afterthought he also gently placed the same old button down shirt on the bed she had worn the last time she slept over. Once finished he returned downstairs, and told her the room was ready for her.

Gail went upstairs and into the room immediately wanting to get through the book as quickly as she could, before Chase had a chance to change his mind. She poured herself a glass of water before lying back on the bed and beginning to read. Downstairs

Chase could easily hear Gail moving about, and then settle down on the bed.

Moving around the house he locked up the doors and made sure the windows were still locked then went back upstairs. Stopping outside of her closed door he lightly knocked.

When she responded without opening the door he said, "I'll be in my room when you're ready for me".

Before turning and walking into his room. As a second thought he went into the office and chose a number of books at random. Taking them back into his room, he lay down on his own bed and read.

Several hours later, Chase was half way through his fourth book when he heard Gail come out of her room and cross the hall. Closing his book around his thumb, he heard her soft knock on the door.

Smiling at her politeness he said, "As promised I'm here for you, if you're ready for me come in and join me".

Gail opened the door wide.

With the door knob still in her hand she said, "I am only part way through the book. It has been an interesting read so far. I was wondering if you would mind if I went downstairs and got something to eat and drink?."

Smiling back at her from his resting place Chase said, "You are welcome to have anything in this house you would like".

Smirking broadly Gail replied, "Oh I intend to take you up on that offer. However at this moment I really could use something to eat and drink. I'll go find myself something then get back into reading the book".

Chase assured her that he was fine with her helping herself to something to eat and drink. He even offered to get it for her. Gail thanked him for the offer but told him she would get it to lengthen her break from reading a little longer to rest her eye's a bit.

Gail went downstairs to the kitchen and found a cold roasted chicken in the refrigerator and decided to have some of it with a few pieces of cheese. She took her time to cut up the chicken and cheese and put it on a plate. As she was putting the chicken and cheese back where she had found them she saw a large pitcher of sweet iced tea.

After a moment's thought she rejected the tea deciding wine would go better with her snack. Gail decided she would get a bottle of wine from the chest the book had been in. She thought it could be another thing she and Chase could share. After all he had been drinking the wine in the chest as he read the book she was now reading. She only thought it would be fitting for her to do the same. She took her snack and a clean wine glass into the living room. The chest was still there. Gail got herself out a bottle of wine and decided to have her snack where she was.

When she had finished her snack there was half of the bottle of wine left. She decided to take it upstairs with her to finish as she continued to read the remainder of the book. As she was walking back into her borrowed room she called back over her shoulder to Chase that she was going back to read, and would see him once she was finished.

Bitter Truths

As the door slowly opened a few hours later, Chase was granted a brief silhouetted view of Gail. To him she had never looked more beautiful. Walking carefully Gail hesitantly entered the room and closed the door behind her. She walked slowly towards the bed trying not to make a single sound. Chase was granted a long look at her bare legs. Sometime during her time in the other room she had stripped off her pants. Chase noticed she had also changed into the old shirt once again. No doubt in an attempt to get comfortable as she read. As such he was granted with a view of her long shapely legs from mid thigh all the way down to her bare feet.

Gail slid onto the bed next the Chase and said, "That was an interesting book, although it was a bit dark and cryptic for my liking. Though after all this time I have finally finished it, I hope you didn't get too bored waiting for me'.

Chuckling Chase assured her that he would never grow bored waiting for her, no matter how long she was.

Smiling at him she said, "I'd hear the rest of your tale if your still willing to share it with me".

Looking at her in disbelief Chase heard her stomach rumble.

Getting up off the bed he said, "Follow me to the kitchen I'll make you something to eat. Then tell you my tale, seeing as your still wanting to hear it".

They made their way to the kitchen in silence. Gail sat at the table as Chase made her a huge meal. He was placing the very last dish on the table, looking into her big bright eyes.

When he began to speak, "This is going to take a while to tell you. If you can please wait until I'm finished to ask me questions. Otherwise it will take me even longer to tell you everything I need to. And I'm sure you will have a good number of questions before I am done.

You've read the book, as I have. However your time with it was different from mine. Before I started reading it I must confess. I had opened a bottle of the wine with it and had started drinking it. Little did I know at the time, the results it would have. Otherwise I would have done things differently. As the book alluded to the wine did change me. I am not the same man you last saw so many months ago. And no before you even begin to think it, I am not now nor have I even been an alcoholic.

Gail felt a pang of horror in the depths of her soul. Chase didn't know it yet, but she had also drunk the wine as she read the book. Looking at him blankly across the table she hoped he wouldn't be too upset with her when she told him. She decided to tell him once he had finished his tale.

I don't want to frighten you, but you need to know exactly how I have changed and what has taken place since that time. I also know you're going to have a hard time believing and accepting all I am about to tell you. But I assure you every single word of it is the god honest truth. Please keep an open mine".

Chase proceeded to tell her of the changes the wine had made in him. Of his other discoveries within the chest, then of the things that had taken place since he had left town. It had taken him six hours to tell her everything he did. He left out everything about hunting and killing humans for their blood. And a few other things that he figured didn't need to be told at present. In order for him to keep his story as short as possible. He would tell her the rest later if she really wanted to know.

As he told her his tale he carefully watched her. Trying to gauge what she was making of it by her facial and body language. Even though she did well, he could see the ever growing sense of horror coming from her. As true to his word his amazing story was a long one and took a long time to tell. That he had talked throughout the remainder of the night, and well into the next day, before he had finished telling her what little of it that he did. Chase made a point of stopping every couple hours for a break, and so she could go home to check on Chase Junior. Each time she left he figured she would not return, but she always did within an hour of leaving.

Chase also stopped at exactly seven p.m., and sent her home as she had told him during one break that was Chase Junior's usual bedtime. He assured her he would resume where he left off when she returned from tucking Chase Jr. in for the night. No matter how long she decided to spend at home with him before returning. Gail had returned to find him waiting where he had been when she left two hours earlier. True to his word he picked up and carried on his story from exactly where he left off. When he was done he merely sat silently, waiting for her to break the silence. She didn't yell, scream or run for the door as he had feared she would. To his amazement she merely stared at him with a mixture of expressions flowing over her face like water. Horror was always the most prominent expression radiating from her. It made Chase's heart sink every time he noticed it.

A long time later Gail reached across the table and picked up Chase's wine glass. Took a long deep drink from it, before very slowly setting it back down in front of him; never taking her eyes off of his the entire time.

Finally she said, "You're right that was quite the tale. And as hard as it all is to believe I have no reason to think you would lie to me about any of it. So you're a vampire. That really isn't all that hard for me to believe. The hard part for me in all of this is that you kept it from me at all. I would like to think that you can trust me enough to keep your secret.

I love you Chase, as I told you before nothing will ever change that. Not even your need to drink blood to survive. All that being said though, I know at present you believe you will outlive me. Now that idea I cannot bear. I am the mother of your child, as you know. That I will never do anything to change either, even if it were within my power to do so; I would not. You will be a father and I will be a mother. As you know he is almost six years old.

Whether you agree with it, or you do not. Not that I can change how you feel, regardless of your choice. I told you I will love you forever, as it seems like forever is now possible, so it will be. We will have our family and figure out all the rest as we go along. It is enough for me for now to have you back by my side. I can carry this secret easily until I become the same creature you are. And then it will be my secret to keep as well".

Chase almost fell out of his chair in amazement with the sheer pleasure of Gail's response and reaction to his tale. For the first time he was happy to of shared his tale with her. He knew it would not be easy for them as they figured things out. But he knew that as long as they were together, they would figure it all out.

They sat at the table talking things over for several more hours. By the time they had finished their conversation, they had made a great deal of decisions. Foremost being that they would find a suitable location to build themselves a suitable home; when the time was right to do so. One that would be large enough for a family of vampires and anyone else that joined them over time. By the time they had finished talking it was nine p.m. Gail surprised him again by informing him that she had told Mackayla that she would be sleeping over. They turned off the lights and locked up as they made their way upstairs to bed.

Laying naked in Chase's large bed, arms and legs entwined Gail leaned closer and kissed him squarely on the lips, laid her head on his chest and said as she drifted off to sleep, "I love you more and more with every passing day, I am happier than you will ever know to be spending eternity with you. Chase I must make a confession of my own to you. I drank a bottle of that wine also as I read the book. I got it when I went downstairs to get something to eat and drink".

Laying her head on his cool chest Gail slipped off to sleep with a smile painted on her face.

Chase lying in the bed with Gail sleeping on his bare chest realized the stark truth in her final words before sleep over took her. As he could feel the warmth fleeing from her body, he realized she had already drawn her final breath.

A.E.

Review Requested:

If you loved this book, would you please provide a review at Amazon.com?

CPSIA information can be obtained
at www.ICGtesting.com
Printed in the USA
LVOW08*2103181116
513628LV00001B/2/P

9 781681 816067